It's Not Easy Being Me

JIMMIE R. MCKNIGHT

Order this book online at www.trafford.com
or email orders@trafford.com

Most Trafford titles are also available at major online book retailers.

Printed in the United States of America.

ISBN: 978-1-4907-1291-8 (sc)
ISBN: 978-1-4907-1293-2 (hc)
ISBN: 978-1-4907-1292-5 (e)

Library of Congress Control Number: 2013915336

Trafford rev. 05/13/2014

www.trafford.com

North America & international
toll-free: 1 888 232 4444 (USA & Canada)
fax: 812 355 4082

I dedicate this book to my mother and father; Jimmie and Lois McKnight

Thank you for helping me to understand that the human experience involves leaving the world a better place than what it was when you came.

Acknowledgements

I would first and foremost like to acknowledge all the students who I have had the opportunity to serve as a teacher. I must acknowledge two outstanding educators Ms. Laura Lee and Mr. Johnny White, Thank You. I would also like to acknowledge Juliet Barnett for the assistance and advice she gave me in editing. I would like to thank my wife, Pamela and my children Christian, Meghan and Ryan for being patient with me during the many days I attempted to write. Lastly, I would like to acknowledge my brother who reminded me to write the novel I always said I wanted to write when we were younger.

Chapter One

FIRST DAY OF SCHOOL

The very first time I saw him, I knew that it was something extraordinary about him. I thought who is this guy? I thought to myself, the kids are going to check him worst than they do me. They are on my case, joking and talking about me every minute; they are really going to joke him. When I say, extraordinary, believe me, there are several outstanding characteristics about Mr. Willis.

First of all, he is extremely short and fat, I mean, husky, fat like a little elf. As this character walked by, I tried to divert my attention from him so I would not have to speak. Moving closer and closer to me, his Earth-shaped head is round, bald, and shines as bright as the moon. Not to mention, he walks with a slight limp. Remembering my experiences with the other boys, I avoided speaking to him, hoping to escape bringing any extra attention to myself. I mean, I want to fit in at Garvey, but to fit in you have to maintain a certain attitude. NO COMPASSION, NO PROBLEM is the image you want to convey. One must act, hard, as if you don't care about anything or anybody. I tell myself I really don't care how people feel, but I still do things to try to fit in. Even when I choose my clothes, I am constantly wondering, what will people think or say about them. Whenever I look in the mirror, I wonder what other people think when they see me.

Unfortunately, it is just like always—my bad luck. I am standing there minding my own business, and the man has to walks up to me, "Excuse me, young man." he states. Without a blink, staring as I think to myself, this guy must shop at the Good Will or some kind of thrift shop, because his clothes are out of style and old looking.

I tried not to stare at the man, but I couldn't help but notice his strange glasses and ugly shoes. See, I seem to always attract people that other people see as outcast or lame. I guess it is something about me. I mean it is crazy, how even in my own head, I don't care about how most people feel. Still something inside me wants to be liked. I mean, sometimes I look at people that everybody else seems to looks up to. Some of them are just mean people, but because they look good, or got money and clothes everybody likes them even if they treat everybody else like they are nothing. Guys like that, are the ones that get all the girls. I sometimes wish that was me. The only exception is that I wouldn't joke people and try to make them feel bad just because I was luckier than them.

I just looked at the man like he was crazy. I mean, he don't know me. Why did he have to choose me out of all people standing with us?

Then Marvin states, "Who are you a substitute or something? Everybody knows the office is soon as you come in the building." The groupies then immediately do their thing and laugh. They only do this because Marvin thinks he is the man. And the followers think they are someone important because they follow him.

Feeling suspicious, I walked toward the direction of the office. I knew Marcus would have something to say. "That's just like a lame, trying to be the teacher's pet," he exclaimed!

The man then paused and looking like a drill sergeant, and stated, "Thank You, young man." Everyone watched as he walked away. Then Marvin and the gang restarted their joking session. "Man, where you get them shoes at? I want some of them. Don't tell me, I know the garbage dump." Instantly the crew starts laughing as another one stated, "Man, he got them from the thrift market."

Next thing I know, everybody started laughing, pointing at my shoes hollering, "Look at Lewis's shoes."

Lorenzo Morris is one of the tallest people at the school. He is actually taller than most freshman or sophomores in high school. He is taller than most of the teachers and has a little hair on his face. Most people can't believe that he is so young. Lorenzo is a true clown. The one thing, he loves to do is talk about people. I think Lorenzo just talks about other people because he is afraid people are going to talk about him. He is in the same situation as I am. He wears old clothes and shoes also. His shoes might be name brand, but they are still old. People just don't talk about him because they are afraid of his height, and they know he will talk about them back. See Garvey is just like the jungle, where the strong and the weak just prey on the weaker or in my case, the weakest.

But I don't let them haters get to me because I know it's not where you start but where you end.

All my life people have talked about me because I don't look good and never had nice shoes or clothes. If I had a million dollars for every time someone called me black, ugly or short. Mama, she tries, but she got me and my younger brother and sister. See my mama made some bad decisions like, moving too fast with Daddy. Daddy and momma grew up in Gordon Homes one of the largest projects in the city. Daddy was sixteen when he met Momma. Momma was only fourteen. Daddy was like a grown man, since he had to take care of his brother and sister. Daddy was smart in school, but he dropped out to help take care of his brother and sister, after his father got shot, at a dice game. Mama's mother was on drugs, and she was practically raised by Grandma, who is in the church. Daddy tried working, but once Mama got pregnant, he felt like he had to get money by any means necessary. Mama said that Grandma tried to warn her, but she was in love with Daddy, so she started with sneaking around with Daddy. Momma always keeps it real with us. She said that she knows they were in love, but they should have waited. Momma said that sometimes it is hard for her to get jobs, because she doesn't have a high school diploma. Momma is very intelligent, but she just doesn't have an education. She said this hurts her, because she can't give us all the stuff we need. Sometimes I do not even want to come to school because I know they are going to joke on me.

I do have one friend, Jason, who lives in the same apartment building as I do. He stays coffin sharp. He is always down with the click in the hood, since he has older brothers. Jason goes to alternative school because he can't seem to do right in our school, which is a step away from that school, so he could just come back here. See, when people joke Jason out, he fights, and I got to give it to him, he does that well. If Jason was going to our school, Marvin and his group wouldn't dare try me like that. Jason and his brothers, they go out and hustle for what they want. Since his brothers are always boosting clothes, Jason has started letting me get a couple of things. Hopefully, this will take some attention off me and stop some of the jokes.

It is kind of messed up that I want to be somebody one day, huh? I mean I just love history and I am good at it. I believe I can be a lawyer one day. I mean look at President Obama. I want to do something with my life, running the street is not going to help me to accomplish my dreams. May be one day I won't be afraid to be me. But they just see me as an ugly boy that walks around, looking like a J as they call it. But it's all good, I still believe in myself. Sometimes I think the joking makes me stronger. It makes me want to work hard. So one day when we get older, and I run into them, they will see what they did, really didn't matter. They are going to be like, what's up Lewis, don't I know you? By then, I will be finished with law school, and the president or at least, a big time lawyer riding in a Benz. I will probably be married to Tiffany, the girl of my dreams, that wouldn't know I existed, unless Trevion hadn't pushed me, on purpose, as he walked by. The shameful incident, I might add, that led to my milk flying everywhere, particularly across the table to land directly on Tiffany. Tiffany just yelled, "Who threw that milk on me?" And of course, everyone yelled my name. When she saw that it was me, she just gave me an understanding look and sat down. I know that doesn't mean Tiffany likes me. But I do know that I love or at least like her a lot. I have written plenty letters, but I am to shy to give them to her. I just keep them in the front part of my book bag. One day I am going to give one to her. Now Tiffany, even though she is beautiful, she does not let it go to her head. She never talks about anybody, and she treats everyone good. She is one of those truly beautiful people inside and out. Tiffany is mild complexioned with long black hair and hazel eyes, sort of like a girls you see in movies. However, she is also known for helping classmates that have problems learning. She is known for speaking to everyone, and treating everyone like they are somebody, whether they are fat, skinny, dress good or bad, smart, or dumb, everyone is a friend. I think a lot of Tiffany's humbleness and nice approach came from her twin sister Tammy. She and Tammy are identical twins. Tammy, however, is autistic. You can always see Tiffany in the cafeteria hugging her sister playing with her. Tiffany and her friends treat her as if she is not autistic. A lot of the treatment Tammy receives is because of the respect people have for Tiffany.

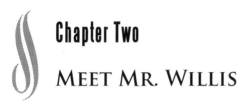

Chapter Two

MEET MR. WILLIS

I walk into the classroom, late as always. That's because I don't like to go to the restroom when the other people are in there. People are always playing, fighting, or joke other people. I will just wait until everyone else starts scrambling to class, and the kids, who are skipping, start hiding in the stalls, and then I use the restroom quickly and try to make it to class before the tardy bell. But, coming to class late is awkward for a shy person like me. I walk in, and instantly all eyes are on me. Just my luck, the man coming down the hall is my teacher, "Young Lady, I apologize, I am sorry, I meant young man. Why are you late?" Of course, this is all the class needs to instantly burst into laughter. I replied quietly, "I had to use the restroom." He stared for a moment and then stated, "Next time try to get to class on time." I sat down embarrassed a little and happy to get out of the spot light. I looked on the board and saw a name, Mr. Willis, so that is his name, I thought to myself. As Mr. Willis began a discussion, he just happened to ask the wrong person a question, Jackie Jones.

Jackie thinks, he is all that. See, Jackie is one of the people considered to have (swag). He always has the top of the line gear on. He always has a fly hair cut, and of course, he looks totally different from how I do, and he can dance. Guess what though, I have figured Jackie out. He really is kind of dumb. So what he will do, is act like he doesn't care, and so then the other kids, since they look up to him, do the same thing. But not me, I am a individual so I just do me whether people like it or not. When Mr. Willis asked him the question, Jackie pondered for what seemed like forever, even though, it was only thirty seconds. He then stated real quickly, "Go to hell." But not like bluntly, but real fast, where only the students, would know what he is saying. What we call a potentially green teacher would just suspect, he said what he said, but wouldn't be able to prove it, without confirming it. So, of course, Mr. Willis stated, "What did you say young man?" Jackie looked somewhat afraid, but he continued laughing and stated, in a nervous and scared voice, "I said, I don't know." Mr. Willis looked at him with a blank face. It seemed, as if he was trying to look inside of Jackie's eyes, like he was trying to figure him out or something. The longer he stared, the greater the chances he would. All of a sudden Jackie breaks the silence, "What are you looking at, you see something you like, or are you going blind?" Mr. Willis's facial expression changed drastically. After a long pause, he took two steps towards Jackie's desk and stated in a forceful but quiet manner, still with the blank expression, "Young Man, stand up. You see this young man. He doesn't understand his work ethic today will impact his reality in the future. He does not understand how much his future depends on what he does today. What do you want to be when you grow up young man?" Jackie paused for a minute, looking around for reinforcement, but seemed to start to get serious when he realized that no one else was laughing. His facial expression went from smiling and smirking, to shame and ducking. Amazing how Jackie loses his confidence when no one is there to back up his show. Now, Jackie shame faced stated, "I don't know, probably a football player, but if that does not work out, I will be a lawyer because they get paid." Mr. Willis then stated, "Son, do me a favor research a famous lawyer. Read his biography, and then come back to me, and tell me what you find. Your research will show that the lawyer went to a prestigious school and studied hard for many years to become a successful lawyer. Before he made it to college, he had to sit in a chair, just as you do. He had to make a decision to pay attention in class, to follow school rules, and avoid following classmates, who made bad decisions. Across from him was another student, when he was your age and grade, who was just as capable and smart that wanted to be a lawyer. This child chose to be disrespectful, not to pay attention in class and disobeyed school rules. He ended up instead of becoming a lawyer, being represented by a lawyer in and out of court for a crime he was charged with. The question is, are you the child that is going to be the lawyer? Or are you the child that is going to need a lawyer?" Jackie looked all around in disbelief and bewilderment and stated, "Oh, I'm going to be something, that's for sure, more than you. I know what I am not going to be, a broke down teacher like you, look at your clothes." Mr. Willis just looked, realizing Jackie was very angry. Jackie then jumped up yelling loudly, "Why are you looking at me? You are not my daddy, what you going to do whip me?" Mr. Green then stormed in, hearing the loud voice from the other room. "Is everything all right Mr. Willis?" He then smiles, and gives Mr. Willis a hug and a secret hand shake. See Mr. Green and Mr. Willis are a part of the same fraternity. Mr. Green is cool with all the kids, and he is younger than the other teachers are, and makes learning fun. Mr. G. is a different type of teacher. He knows how to relate to the students. Mr. Willis then gives him a reassuring smile and states, "Everything is all right brother, I have a young brother that needs a little grooming." Mr. Green looks over eye to eye with Jackie and states, "Jackie are you being disrespectful towards Mr. Willis?" Jackie pauses for a second, considering wether to try the same antics with Mr. Williams and states in a quiet mild like manner, "No, Mr. Green I was just kind of angry, it want happen again." Mr. Green and Mr. Willis then walked out of the room discussing old times.

Chapter Three

THE CHARACTERS AT GARVEY MIDDLE SCHOOL

W e are in the boy's room. Now for those of you who don't know, that's where everything goes down. That's where all the fights break out, plans get discussed, and most of all, lies get told. Even though they have teachers out in the hall, most teachers want even go in the boys' restroom. The smell along, would knock you out. The minute you hit the door, you can smell the aroma of wet urine. It's amazing, how even with that smell, you can almost always find boys camped out, during time change, on top of toilets. For some reason, these boys hope they will make it pass the tardy bell without being caught, so they can hang in the bathroom.

Because of all the fights, the security guards make rounds during rotations to class. But the bad boys are smarter than they are given credit for. If the boys know the guards are about to go in the restroom, it would be just like the prison yard. One group of people will do something to divert Mr.

Lee, the security guard's attention. Often, it is girls, who are groupies that run out of the restroom screaming down the hall. This will temporarily cause Mr. Lee to run to the other side of the hall. This will allow the rumble to start. It usually ends with someone getting beat down. Walking out of the restroom with their pride hurt and smelling like urine, the other students, then will scramble out into the hall to joke about what happened as the gossip girls wait to get the story and immediately pass it through the hall. This, often time, follows with all the teachers rushing to the halls to try to redirect students to class.

The restroom is also a prime place for joking along with the other illegal transactions and behaviors taking place. Since I am a prime target, I normally try to dodge the restroom during class change. But today I couldn't hold it and I know Dr. Grant told me if I come in her office again for being late, she is going to give me ISS. In addition, I don't want ISS because that's like being in solitary confinement in jail. As soon as I walk in the restroom I hear Melvin talking,

"Did you see that new teacher; he looks like a fat dwarf? If I was that ugly, man, I swear I would carry a bag over my face." Melvin stated, as he continued to comb his nappy hair. I wanted to say, if my hair was as nappy as yours, I would just cut it off. I mean it's evident that Melvin don't ever comb his hair, and then he wants to try to put on a front as if, he combs his hair when he gets to school. Richard then stated," Come on man, do not talk about the brother, he seems like a good brother." All he is trying to do is enlighten us, young brothers." "With the ugly thrift store clothes he got on, Mr. Willis can't tell me a thing, except for how not to be like his J looking self."

Richard is different from most students. He has both of his parents in the home. In addition, he is into that Muslim stuff, so his father does not play. Richard and his brothers know not to get out of line. But all of them have a reputation for being tough. Don't get me wrong, they don't bully people, but when you come to them, you better come correct. So they don't pick on him or joke him to much, like they do me.

The second period bell rings, and I grab my books and head to class. Just before class, Malcom, Jeremy, and I will normally meet to trade video games and share homework. We are not friends or anything, but because they are kind of outcast like me, we seem to just deal with each other. In the front of me is Leah. Leah is what you would call a little, hot mother. She wants to be grown before her time. She comes in the school dressed like a grown woman. She always has on something tight or short, to show more of her thick/fat portions. "I can't stand her little boogie self. I am going to get a chance to pull all her hair out of her head before the school year gets out." She stated as she played with the gum in her mouth, with that devious look; she normally has on her face. You cannot tell Leah she is not fine, she thinks because she looks older for her age, all the boys want her. However, she is really the type of girl that boys only like because they know she is down for whatever. "What are you looking at, ugly?" Leah directs with attitude my way.

Leah and I have sort of a history due to an incident. She and Tiffany had been enemies since last year, when they were both talking to Marcus. Leah and Tiffany were running for queen. The election basically came down to the people who hated Tiffany because they were jealous because she gets high grades, and all the boys like her, as well as, the teachers. Therefore, when Tiffany came out with her nice posters and placed them with a picture of her all around the school, that was all that Leah and her crew could take. They then came up with a plan to tear down the posters early that morning. They planned for everything. They knew that the janitors were on morning duty. All they had to do is have two friends stay near the janitors, while the other two are on the other halls tearing down posters. The only problem with the plan is that I was hungry as hell that day. We did not have any food at home. All I ate that night for dinner was old stale noodles.

Because I was hungry that morning I came to school early to get breakfast. So as I am waiting on the cafeteria doors to open, I saw Leah and her crew walking in but they did not see me. I just followed them to the corner. A couple of minutes later, they came out with hats pull down. So I followed them, and I saw them running through the halls, ripping down posters, tearing them in half. When everyone got to school, the principal, security and the janitors couldn't believe the destruction. The principal and the security were lost as usual. They instantly begin calling in the usual suspects. They started their interrogation methods, which only made the usual suspects happy, because they got to laugh and say they did not do it. They love to get the bad kid attention that helps them to keep their image. It's weird how some people take pride in getting in trouble and the reputation that goes with it. Of course, I had a bit of a problem. Know one wants to be a snitch, no matter how much you may dislike the person you could snitch on. However, when I saw how sad Tiffany looked that morning and when she burst into tears and ran out of the room, I did not have a choice. There was no way I could see her hurt and not come to her rescue. When she cried that day, it was like I could feel her pain.

So I did the right thing and told the principal what happened. Leah and the crew, as I like to call them, were now my enemies for life. They took every opportunity they could to ridicule me and make my life miserable. Tiffany, at least from that point on became my guardian angel. When she was around, no one could pick on me without her butting in to scold them and make them shame of their actions. See, Tiffany could get away with that, since she is like the most popular girl in the school.

Since then Leah and crew has done everything she could to make my life miserable. She and the crew would just wait for me sometimes to come into the school and joke me. It got so bad I wanted to skip school, but I thought to myself, if people talked about Jesus, I know they are going to talk about me. To tell the truth, Leah and her friends are kind of amateurs at insulting people. I have been being called ugly, black and so much more that it doesn't faze me as much. But they seem to try to calculate their attempts at humiliating perfectly. It's always done at a moment which is extremely public to maximize the embarrassment like the cafeteria and hall. They always ensure that their insults will divert all attention towards me. Today was a classic example Leah hollered out sarcastically, "Know that's a true Junkie, look at those shoes!! What kind of trash, I mean, shoes are those?" As she and all her friends pointed at my shoes. Everyone immediately began to laugh loudly. I feel like I want to crawl in a dark hole and never come out.

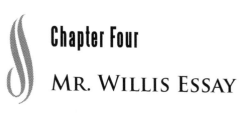

Chapter Four

MR. WILLIS ESSAY

Mr. Willis finally walks in as the bell rings and the class instantly becomes quiet. Mr. Willis then asks everyone to take out a pencil or pen and his or her notebooks. "Everyone please take a moment to reflect. I would like each student to write a brief essay. The essay should discuss why it is important to get an education. I am setting the timer, you have ten minutes." The students pause as Mr. Willis looks across the room constantly making eye-to-eye contact with each student. The class then begins to write. They instantly start to debate about education, and how dumb this journal reflection is. Everyone knows that people get an education, so that they can make money and have a better life. This can be summed up in one to two sentences. So this leaves me with the rest of the time to day dream. The timer finally goes off, after what seems like an eternity. Mr. Willis looks around the room gazing at each student like an FBI agent trying to discern the truth. Can anyone tell me why they think it's important to get and education?

Suddenly, the class "Know-IT-ALL" Kevin Woods raises his hand; "I choose to get and education so that I can follow in my father and grandfather's footsteps and attend Morehouse College. Education is important to prepare me for my future as a medical doctor." Kevin is lucky, unlike most kids; he has both his father and his mother in the house with him. In addition, his mother is a state senator and his father is a doctor. Children do not really bother Kevin for being a "know-it-all" because he dresses very well, and all the girls like him. They like Kevin because he has that pretty boy look. You know light skinned with the curly hair. After Kevin's response people then began to answer with their responses. They mostly talked about the usual, big cars and nice houses, and described educations as a means towards possibly acquiring the finer things in life. Mr. Willis just listened as if in deep thought, as he looks around the room. Lewis he then stated "Let me hear your reflection."

I then began to read,

"I think getting an education is important because it will allow you to get the skills necessary to get a good job. This will allow me to help my mother and my siblings. I also think getting an education is important, because if I drop out, my brothers and sisters may follow in my foot steps and drop out. Getting an education will allow me to grow up and not have to struggle and work low paying jobs. However, most of all getting an education will allow me to live out my dreams. Education is as important to me, as the air I take to breathe, because it gives me life too."

I instantly wanted to just run out of the classroom because I can just imagine the jokes people are going to have about my reflection. Mr. Willis then began to smile as he pondered his next words before stating, "I remember when I had to answer the question for myself, why get and education? I guess I was around twelve. Twelve, when I started to question, why it was important to get and education. I remember the teacher would tell us that we should study hard because too many people had fought and died to give us an opportunity at an education. I also was told that you get and education not so you can make money, but so you can contribute to society and make lives better for yourself, as well as other people. Therefore, I rather agree with Lewis that education should be based on the overall goal you have for your life. You should want to get an education so that you can give yourself options and choices."

William, the joker as I call him, raises his hand. I instantly know that he is about to say something to try to get the entire class to erupt in laughter. "Mr. Willis, do you have an education?" Mr. Willis replies, "Yes". William looks around with a devious smile then states, "If you have an education and this is type of job you do, I don't want one. You got an education, and look at you, you work at Garvey." Mr. Willis stared at William as if he is dissecting everything he said, and then states, "That's true, I teach at Garvey, but, before I taught here, I worked in Washington as a political consultant. Before working in Washington, I was an officer in the military. Before joining the military, I was in the Peace Corps. I have had the opportunity to travel and live in many of the nations that I am teaching you about. The reason I am teaching now is that I happen to enjoy teaching and find it rewarding. But, I always have the option to pursue other interest."

Mr. Willis then asks everyone to take out a sheet of paper to take a test. The room instantly fills with murmuring and low complaints. Mr. Willis quieted the class by stating in a reassuring manner, "Don't worry, it is not going in the grade book, it's just a short test to see what you already know so I can know what you need to know."

Chapter Five

NEW SHOES OLD CLOTHES

The minute I walk through the door mother is waiting for me. She informs us with the sad news that she didn't get the hours she was supposed to last week. This meant that we wouldn't get the new clothes she promised us. My mother works part-time at Vikings Chicken, but she is sometimes able to get full time hours. My father was arrested for robbery and aggravated assault; I was six when my father was arrested. He has been in jail as long as my sister and brothers can remember. I have been the (so-called man) of the house since. However, even though my daddy is in jail, he found the lord and tries to be a good father from jail. He always sends us these letters, discussing church and stuff. He always tells us to remember to pray and do the right thing and good things will happen. My mama tries her best, so I try not to stress her about buying expensive stuff because I know she can't afford it. She did promise us some new clothes and shoes when she got her income taxes, but her hours have been cut these last few weeks. This means momma had to use the tax money to pay the rent, but even though mama didn't have the money to buy us clothes, she still agreed to buy us a pair of shoes and took us to the Good Will to get a couple of outfits. I was so excited about the shoes I could hardly sleep at night. The minute I walk in the school the jokers immediately notice my new shoes. Some kid, name Richie, yelled out, "I guess, even Junkies can get new shoes?" People immediately burst out into laughter.

When I walked into Mr. Willis's class, he had already started giving out the assignment. Even though people like to joke on me, usually they want me in their groups because I am a good student. They want me to do all the work while they sit, talk, text, and do everything else, except the assignment. Mr. Willis is aware of these tricks and decides that he is going to choose the groups. Just my luck, I end up in the group with Leah, one of her friends, and Marcus. I instantly know that there is going to be some type of conflict by the resentful eye; I get from my group members, as we take our seats. Leah instantly starts to protest, "Mr. Willis, why can't we choose our own groups? I do not want to work with that little boy!" Mr. Willis states, "I understand, you don't want to work with Lewis, but let me give you a scenario. One day you are going to be an adult and have a job. There are going to be some people, whose personality or swagger, as you all like to say, you just don't get along. You will still need to find a way to work together to get the task accomplished. Well, that is the same thing in the classroom. You may not like each other, but you must be willing to work together to accomplish a common goal. So just look at this as a life-lesson."

The other person in our group, Leah's friend Tamar, is sort of a school celebrity. She is a very talented dancer. Her mama has had her in ballet since she was two. When I say the girl got moves, this girl has moves. She is always being asked to dance at the school for plays and assemblies and all the mega churches around the city. Just recently, she was even asked to dance at the mayor's inauguration.

Any way, Mr. Willis asks the class to imagine if they could travel back in time to any place in the world or time period. Mr. Willis then asked us to write a diary of what their experiences would be at the place. Marcus opens his big-fat mouth instantly to complain. You know he is the type that no matter what the assignment is, he is going to complain and try to get out of completing it.

Mr. Willis pauses for a moment as if he is really attempting to come up with—an answer.

Mr. Willis then states "I want you to see that this world and environment that you see today is only temporary, and that, a whole great world is out there for you to explore and enjoy."

Mr. Willis takes a sigh, and then states, "When you were little, you always watched television and cartoons and envisioned you were someone else. "Imagine being born at a different time or life. How different would that impact the way you view life to be Marcus Garvey or Hannibal of Carthage?"

"Marcus Garvey is lame, who wants to be like him?" Mr. Willis looked at the student and stated, "Why do you feel this way towards Mr. Garvey?" Joshua then stated, "I feel that Mr. Garvey should not have tried to send us back to Africa, but instead. I think we should focus on fighting for our rights in this country." Mr. Willis then stated, "I see your point, but this is just an exercise to practice your writing."

As we started the exercise, at first, I was thinking, I am going to just wait to see what the rest of the group is going to do. After a while, I can see from the, "you all ready know" look of Leah that I am on my own. If I want to get a good grade on this project, I will have to take all the roles of the group. That became instantly true with the role of Leah's eyes, indicating you already know you had better get to work. Lisa and her crew began a conversation about how bad other girls in the class, hair and clothes look as I attempted to think about what I am going to write.

I imagined myself as a child during the Alabama boycotts. I imagined I was one of the children jailed with Dr. King.

Dear Momma,

I am so afraid in this jail. I hear the guards yell all kind of racist words such as the n word. But we just keep on singing songs. Most of the days we talk about what our plans are for the next march. The guards look at us like we are crazy. They can't understand how we can be so happy and ready to get back in a line to be humiliated, beaten, and arrested. But I am happy about the future because I believe that one day my little sister and brother will be able to get treated like a human. Sometimes late at night I get lonely though and I wish Mamma and Daddy was here.

I feel like a hero because I know we are doing something to save the world.

Today it is raining; I know that God's tears are raining down on the world for the misery and sorrow that our people have had to endure. But even though it is gloomy and cold outside our souls are full of sunshine. This morning I create a new song, "Want be Long Now" because I know it want be long now before the sun will shine on all of us.

I read the journal entry to Lisa and she wanted to know what made me choose something so sad. I told her about how my father, even though he is in jail, he taught me about the struggle people went through to give us equal opportunities at education. He also told me that even in bondage you can still be free.

Mr. Willis then chose groups to read their assignments. All I could do was pray that my group is not called. I guess Leah could read my mind because she raised her hands wildly to try to get Mr. Willis's attention. Just my luck Mr. Willis decided to call on our group.

Instead of Leah using this as an opportunity to put me on the spot, she decided to steal the show. Leah jumped up and presented our assignment as if she had written the assignment herself.

Mr. Willis then stated with an excited smile, Excellent job Leah. You and your group did an excellent job." She looked at me with a devious smile and then stated, "Thanks, Mr. Willis".

Leah knows she could have said something to let Mr. Willis know how hard I worked on that diary writing. She smirked as she walked off, whispering under her breath, "I guess your ugly self is good for something." I wanted to say something negative about Leah, but I decided to ignore her this time.

Chapter Six

CONQUERING THE BULLY

Now here I am walking down the hall minding my own business. Just like always, trouble finds me. Marvin, a known bully, bumps into me. I looked at him surprised and shocked and instantly I stated, "My bad man, excuse me." Marvin being the person he is, had to overreact. Marvin looked at me mean and pushed me as he stated, "Why did you bump into me, boy?" I don't really like to fight, especially someone bigger than me, but I didn't want to look scary, so I pushed Marvin back. At this point, people began to crowd around. At first we stood their exchanging threats for about thirty seconds. As the crowd grew larger, I heard people yelling, "Man punch him, man." "Fight", People then began to yell fight. And of course, Marvin decided to throw the first punch, and the next five punches for that matter. One of the punches caught me in the eye and instantly I saw stars. After that, all I could do was run towards his body as he punched me. I tried to grab him but had no luck. The next thing I knew, security rushed in as I held my head down, while blood trickled from my nose. All I could see as security escorted me to the office was people pointing and yelling excitedly, "Man, Marvin beat him down." I heard a couple of people in the crowd yelling insults as they pointed laughing. As I walked by, I could see Tiffany watching with a sad look. For some reason, once I saw her, I forgot about everything. As I gazed in her eyes, I could see she was not entertained by my beat down, like the rest of the crowd. This made me feel even more embarrassed, I am getting beat down in front of the girl I like.

I was so embarrassed; I started running as I turned the corner going towards the next hallway. Mr. Willis was turning the corner at the same time. I tried to hold back the tears, as they flowed from my face slightly as blood trickled from my nose. I tried to hold back my tears as I walked down the hall. I was so embarrassed. I wish I could just zap myself and leave the school.

Mr. Willis walked over he then stated, "Young man, what's wrong?" Are you Ok?" Mr. Willis calmly stepped in front of me. "Calm down young man, walk with me for a minute." By then security had ran up. Mr. Willis then asked the security guard to allow him to walk me to the principal's office. As we walked, Mr. Willis began another one of his stories. He told how when he was young, he had got in a fight where he was beat up pretty bad. Even though he was embarrassed he held his head up, and after time people forgot about the fight.

As we walked, it was hard to keep up with the long fast walking of Mr. Willis, but by the time I made it to the principal's office, I felt a little better. Also, I knew that Mr. Willis was not just a teacher, but a teacher that cares.

Chapter Seven

MOMMA MEETS MR. WILLIS

The minute momma found out about the fight, she was, of course, disappointed to say the least. She went on and on about the Bible and how I was taught to turn the other cheek and walk away. She went on about how I should be setting an example for my sister and brothers. She knew that saying that hurt me worse than any punishment she was about to give.

She couldn't really punish me like she wanted to, since I have to keep my sister and brothers when she is at work. Momma had to go to school after my suspension ended. Mrs. Young, the counselor, informed me and Momma that Mr. Willis had agreed to be my mentor. Mr. Willis and Momma agreed that I would clean halls before connections for a week and report to him daily with my agenda so he could keep up with my progress.

Mr. Willis feels like I have potential. He actually believes I can attend college. In my family, no one has every finished college, only a few people have finished high school. He told my momma that there was a need for a mentor to keep me from going the wrong way.

Momma agreed with Mr. Willis that I had potential. I was kind of embarrassed to hear her talk about our economic problems, and how she struggled as a single mom. She talked about how I have to keep my sister and brothers and raise them while she is at work.

Momma and Mr. Willis talked for a long time. I could tell Mr. Willis made a good impression on Momma and that she liked him.

"We need more teachers at that school like Mr. Willis." Teaching is like preaching, it has to be a calling. He is not one of those pay check teachers that's for sure."

I told momma how all the students think he is weird and how they laugh at how he dresses. But, his class is always fun and everyone learns. I couldn't understand why this man cared so much about students that most teachers called statistics, which are going to be dead, on welfare or in jail in the future anyway.

Momma just smiled and said, "I wouldn't worry about why, I would just listen to a wise man."

Momma didn't want to hear me say no as an answer in relations to Mr. Willis's idea. I was told that I had to do it, or I was really going to regret it, and you know what that means. So I didn't have a choice but to do it, but I definitely don't feel comfortable having a teacher watching your every move. But it would be kind of cool to have someone to talk to about this crazy life.

After a day or so of working with Mr. Lewis and then reporting to Mr. Willis, on today Mr. Willis was waiting when I walked in and stated, "Where is your journal, for today?"

He then checked to view every teacher's response, asking me about each class. He saw that all my teachers had good things to say about my performance and behavior, except in math. In math, I failed to complete the assignment. "What's your problem with math?" he asked. I see you did well in all your other classes, as you did in my class." "I don't understand how to do the problems, and I can't understand Ms. Patrick." Mr. Willis then paused, "I tell you what, I am going to enroll you in tutorial." Also, I am going to speak with Malik and ask him to help you. He is a good student in math. But in exchange, I am going to ask you to help him in Social Studies and Language Arts. Young people have got to learn to work together, and pool your talents to increase your ability to succeed."

Chapter Eight

BOOSTING FOR CLOTHES

Momma has not mentioned my fight every since I started working with Mr. Willis. Today is a regular Saturday, and Jason and I are hanging out. I am glad momma is not mad at me. This means Jason and I can go to the skate party.

Jason likes to come by my house and get on the computer since they don't have one. It's crazy how they have this big flat screen TV. and a nice Escalade, but they do not have a computer. Momma might not have a car, but at least we have the internet. Momma said she would always come up with money to pay for us to have unlimited access to knowledge at our hand. I don't know about unlimited knowledge, but I love being able to get on face book and the other social websites.

Momma did tell us that we couldn't get on the computer without her being there. But I figured she wouldn't know. Jason was on face book checking his messages. Jason is what you call, a ladies' man. He is not shy like me. When I get around girls, sometimes I don't know what to say. My heart starts to beating fast and my hands get sweaty, especially around Tiffany.

Jason and I are totally different. He's big for his age and mature for his age since he hangs around his older brothers. Jason got in a lot of trouble last semester, because of this; he has to go to alternative school this semester. Momma lets me hang around Jason because I don't really have any friends, and Jason is always nice around Mama. He says yes sir and no sir, which always gets adults respect. Jason actually is smart. He just has a quick temper and will do anything for money. Jason never missed class and always paid attention in class, but when some guys decided to steal a lap top, Jason went with them. Jason didn't let that get him down. Jason has big dreams. "Man I am telling you, I am going to play for the Falcons one day. I am going to be a running back and a lawyer. I might even buy you a Benz."

Prior to last year, Jason and I were together every minute, but now he spends all his time playing park league football and hanging with his brother and their friends.

Jason has been on the computer for over an hour probably posting to replies on facebook. "Jason, get off the computer man," I yelled down the hall. Jason then yelled back, "Give me a few minutes." I started to pick up my video games.

I looked in the mirror to see that the swollen eye from the fight is barely noticeable. Momma said I got my determination from my father, which makes me not want to give up. Also, I have my Daddy's big nose and brains.

Before daddy went away I didn't feel like I do now. It's like my world ended. I no longer felt safe, I was forced to think like a man, but I knew I was still a boy. That kind of took away my confidence. When Daddy was around, we didn't have to worry about much. Even though we didn't have much money, we just felt safe.

Every since Daddy got locked up, Momma seems like she lost something. Even though Daddy tried to give me advice, it's hard for him to tell me something when he is in jail. We are struggling. It's like when I talk to him I can see his pain. Deep down, I know he is angry at himself, but he is ashamed that his children have to suffer because of his mistakes.

Every time we go to see Daddy, he always ends with mumbling advice and shameful looks with the same quote, "Be a man, son, I made many mistakes. The saddest thing in the world is missed opportunity. You are my second chance. I am depending on you to do the right thing. I messed up, you are my second chance. Keep God first, and everything will be all right." I guess he always says that last, because he wants us to keep those things in mind.

Jason is on the internet checking out the videos. All of a sudden I had an idea, "Man, I think I might start rapping. Then I can get paid like the rappers."

Jason jumps off the computer yelling, "You need to get like Big Mo and start trapping skip rapping." Big Mo is like the president in our hood. Big Mo was a star basketball player in high school. He ended up getting hurt in college and started selling drugs. He didn't go pro but he became a legend in the hood for his hustling skills in the streets.

I walked over to the mirror to look at my hair. "Man, I'm about to cut my hair." Jason looked at me like I was crazy. "Man, don't mess your hair up, I remember when Larry tried to cut his hair. He tried to wear a hat, but the teachers made him take it off. People made jokes about his hair all day. He didn't come to school for three days after that. We can go to

Big Joes's barber shop and sweep hair, and they will cut your hair."

Jason and I went down to the barbershop. When we walked in, everyone, of course, knew Jason. All the men were like what's up, J. We stayed up there about three hours listening to men talk about sports and women, as we swept up hair. Jason and I decided to get Mohawks like the rapper Golden Boy. Lonnie, the barber, looked at my head and decided to add a part to give it that extra swag.

Jason and I were turned-up because now we get to go to the skating ring with fly hair cuts. On the way home Jason told me to walk with him to the shopping center. I agreed to go since we had to pass that way anyway. Just my luck, a couple of guys from Jason's brother's crew were there.

"What's up J? Man, what are you getting into?" "Nothing much man," J stated. The two boys looked at J and then stated with a smirk, "You already know what time it is." I instantly knew they were up to something. Jason looked at me, "Man just wait outside for us."

The minute they said that I knew that I should have started walking home. However, I felt like Jason is my friend and besides, he is always giving me clothes. In addition, I did not want to look like I was scared. Jason and the other boys went into the store and I just stood their waiting. Normally it would not have been a big deal. Jason and the boys would normally, from what he told me, just grab a few shirts and hide them under their shirts. I do not know what went wrong, but the next thing I know, about fifteen minutes later, I see Jason and the other boys running with a hand full of stuff. I was just shocked. I did not know whether to run or to just stand there. All of a sudden, I see the police pull up as Jason and the boys escaped through the pathway into field. The store owner by that time runs over to me, "Just stay right here son, you are only going to make it worse on yourself." As I looked confused, looking around for Jason. How? I don't know, but Jason and the boys got away. This meant that I was holding the bag while the police and manager began to interrogate me. The officer asked, "Were you with those boys?" I then stated, "No." He then paused watching me to see if I was lying before stating, "Do you know them?" I paused for a moment thinking if I lie about knowing them he probably wouldn't believe me. Yes, I know them, but I wasn't with them. The officer then looked at the store manager to see his opinion, the owner immediately stated, "I believe he was with them I think they all came in together." The officer looked over at me and then stated, "Where were you coming from?" I then replied quickly, "I was working at the barbershop down the street." The officer then asked, "So was anyone with you when you left the barber shop?" I looked sad and paused for a moment and then stated, "No one left the barbershop with me. But my friend, Jason was at the barber shop with me during the day, but he went to the China King, three streets down." The officer then looked at me and the manager, as if he was not buying my story and stated, "I tell you what. I will drive him back to this barber shop and speak with the barbers to find out, if what he is saying is true. If that's true, I will just drive him home. But if you see any of those boys again, don't hesitate to call me." The police then escorted me to the car. The ride back to the shop must have been the longest ride of my life. All I could think of was how disappointed Momma was going to be.

When we made it back to the shop, the officer walks out and speaks with the owner. I don't know what the owner said, but he just looked at me and continued to speak with the officer. The officer paused and looked my way for a brief moment and started to walk back towards the car as I awaited my doom, "Looks like you are in luck today, the owner said you left less than an hour ago. I guess I can drop you off at home." The officer then began to drive. I thought about it for a minute then I realized, if Momma saw a police car drop me off and heard a story like that, regardless of what he says, she is still going to find me guilty. As we pulled up to the apartment I quickly stated, "Officer, you can drop me off in the front, if you don't mind." The officer hesitated for a moment, "Are you sure you don't want me to drop you off?" I then looked at him nervously with bucked eyes, Oh I'm sure. I'm sure, alright enough."

The minute I make it to the apartment, I started straight to Jason's house. Jason looks out the window, as if he is an animal being preyed. "What's up, man? Wait one minute, I'll be right out?" I waited. And then, Jason realizing, the heat is not on him and starts laughing. Me, I don't get what's funny at all. Jason then states, "Man, did you see us dip on that police officer? We were gone before they could call back-up. Man you have to see all the stuff I grabbed." I looked at Jason like he was crazy. "Man do you know I almost went to jail? I don't ever want to be around you when you do that again." Jason grabbed me still laughing. "You chill bro; I got some fresh gear for you. I promise, next time we do something like that I want involve you."

Chapter Nine

SKATING RING WITH NEW CLOTHES SWAG

I make sure my bedroom door is locked and pull the designer clothes from under my bed and throw them on. I can't wait until tonight. People want even recognize me with the new hair cut and clothes. Tonight is locking-in party at Skate World and Momma told me I can go. The lock in is, about 9:00 the doors are locked and the skating ring becomes a dance floor. I throw on my designer shirt and jeans along with my shades. I looked in the mirror and I instantly began to feel like a new person. New clothes boost your swag. They make me feel like I a famous rapper or something. I then peaked out the window. This is now an army mission, I have to figure out a way to get out of this small apartment without alerting momma. I took my brother and sister to the kitchen, and I gave them those cookies I bought yesterday. I knew they would be still eating. I waited until I heard Momma go into her room, before I left out of my room. Normally, if she has just gotten off work, she goes into her room to take a nap. This gives me a chance to get away. "Good bye, momma, I'll see you when I get back." Momma is always worried when I go out at night. In our neighborhoods, we have two drug houses. One is a candy woman house, where you can also buy a blunt. Even though the police constantly circle the neighborhood, you can still occasionally hear gunshots at nighttime. Momma quickly yells back, "Make sure you only go to the skating ring." The minute I make it outside the skating ring, everyone is gathered in one spot in the complex. I can see Jason in the middle, telling everyone a story. Jason is so excited that I did not tell the police on him, even when I was caught. Jason started smiling as he noticed me walking up and stated, "Man, I don't care what anybody say, L is my boy. I know he down with me, no matter what." We stand their talking for a minute. I am just glad, I finally feel accepted by everyone. We then headed to the skate party. Once we made it there, Jason, his brothers and the rest, some other guys from the hood, then started to party. They represented our little click, or should I say their click, since I am not a part of it, technically. I am only hanging out with them because Jason and I are friends. As they started to dance all around, I instantly go back to being me, which means trying to become invisible in the corner wishing Tiffany would notice me. As I do my usual post on the wall, all of a sudden, Marvin, the guy who I got to fighting with, walks up. He is with a group of guys from his hood, and they all stop right in front of me. I tried to ease off, but it's too late, he just noticed me. Wanting to prove how much swag he has at my expense, he walks up to me. "You see his eye, that's what happens when you try me." His entire click then starts laughing, as he points at me proudly. I start to walk off as the boys in his click point, when out of nowhere, Jason walks up. "What's up L, man are these some of your friends from school?" The guy then looks at Jason, in confusion. I glanced over at the guy and his click and put my head down. Jason then walks up. "What's up, my name is J and anybody cool with L is cool with me. This guy looks at the rest of the guys in his click with a slight hint of fear and states, "What if he is just a lame to us that just got beat down?" Jason then paused and looked around as if he can't believe what he is hearing and states, "If that's the case man, I am telling you, we got major problems." I instantly knew that things were going to get out of hand. Before I could try to calm Jason down, they were fighting. The next thing I know, all of Marvin's boys from his hood started rushing in. Jason hit the first boy knocking him to the ground. He then grabbed Marvin and slammed him to the ground. As Jason began punching him, another kid tried to sneak Jason from the back. I then ran over and grabbed the kid by the neck and began punching him. Jason then turned around and punched him one time knocking him out too. People were getting hit with chairs and everything. I look up and about ten or fifteen people are fighting as crowds of people watched. Girls were jumping back to avoid being hit, and you could see people with phones holding them up attempting to record the fight. I can see Jason and another boy from the complex just kicking Marvin as he starts to hide his face. The fight that probably lasted about two minutes seemed like two hours. Finally, security came rushing in and people started scrambling for the door. I thought I would be able to get away, but the police instantly pointed out everyone involved in the fight and directed them towards his car. The officers called all of our parents up to the skating ring to pick us up. While I waited, all I could think was man, I really let Momma down. I know she is going to be disappointed. She just talked to me about being a man and a leader for my sister and brothers, and I go and do something like this. About an hour later momma pulls up. She had to pay one of the neighbors next door to bring her up to the skating ring with the children, so I know she is going to be mad. The officer explained to momma what happened. He also said that a case would be filed since one of the boys was injured and had to go to the emergency room. The whole time I am just looking with my head down, as Momma looks at me with a disappointing stare that made me want to die. As we rode home, the neighbor consoled Momma, the best she knew how. I do not think Momma was feeling her stories of her sons going in and out of jail. Momma didn't want to imagine that being me.

The minute we got home, we put the kids to bed. Then momma just sat down and started crying with her head down. Momma looked so sad I felt like dying. I walked over and tried to hug her as she cried. "Momma, don't cry, I am sorry, I didn't mean to hurt you. I didn't try to get in a fight it just happened." Momma looked up at me with tears in her eyes, "Son, I have always put my all in trying to raise you right. I know where the stuff you getting into now can lead to. I don't know what to do. I don't want to see you dead or behind bars." I didn't know what to do or say. Momma seemed like she was going crazy, so I just went and grabbed Grandpa's old Bible. "Momma I know I am not supposed to swear, but I promise you, I want ever let you down anymore like I did tonight! I promise, Momma!" Momma then looked up at me and started hugging me. Then she stated, "I am just worried about you son. I want you to break that chain in our family. I want you to finish high school and not go to prison."

Chapter Ten

THE CONFLICT CONTINUES

Monday as I walked into school I expected everyone to be scoping me out for two reasons. First, I got on all new gear, and I am looking good for a change. I had to sneak the clothes out of the house and change in the cafeteria. The last thing I need right now is for Momma to find those clothes. I don't know what she would do if she found out about me being involved in boosting clothes, along with the fights. I don't even know what's happening. One minute I was a kid that hadn't ever been in trouble, and now, all of a sudden, trouble seems to be around every corner. It's funny, but when I walk in the cafeteria, I kind of feel proud. Here it is today; I don't have to feel bad about my clothes or getting beat up. Today I got on the best clothes and the super swag cause me and my crew beat up Marvin. The minute I walk in the cafeteria people started walking up to me speaking and stuff. Normally, the only time people say something to me is to joke and try to make me feel bad about how I look or dress or whatever else they can think of to say. I guess word got around about what happened at the skating ring. You know it only takes a couple of seconds for people to start texting and gossiping on face book and posting pictures. I walk over to the area I normally sit in. This normally was me and a couple of other guys, who don't really fit in, sit. We normally just talk about video games and stuff like that. All of a sudden I see Marvin and the friends come in. I instantly loose my appetite. I quickly put my tray up and slid through the side door down the hall safely to my class. I knew that my getting away in the cafeteria was just lucky, and that they would soon catch up to me. They didn't want to fight in the cafeteria anyway, because it is too much security. They would probably get a few punches in before it was broken up. I thought about it, maybe I should just go to the counselor, but instead I decided to go on to class. By the end of homeroom, I walk towards Mr. Willis and it's just my luck, Marvin and his crews are waiting. I didn't have a choice at this point but to attempt to walk into the class. The next thing I know Marvin was in my face yelling, "Yeah, you and your boys jumped us Saturday, what's up now? This time I wasn't going to let him sneak me. I rushed towards him slamming him against the door. I slammed him into it so hard, that the door cracked. Mr. Willis came running out and grabbed us as we were about to fight. I knew I was in a world of trouble. I don't know what was going through my head. I just got scared. I didn't want to get beat up like last time. Mr. Willis looked at me with disappointment, "I can not believe you two are still continuing to go on with this foolishness. You two just don't learn."

Mr. Walker, the security guard, then walked up and escorted us to the principal's office. The principal decided to call our parents and inform them we had to pay for the broken glass. He also gave each of us in-school suspension. As we waited on our parents to show up, the principal sent us up to the Counseling office. We were escorted in to speak with Mrs. Mims, normally I was always glad to go to her office. Just to see her brought a smile to my face. Miss. Mims is what you call a true dime. She has long pretty hair and bronze skin that looks like shining brass. Ms. Mims always has on something which shows off her perfect Coca-Cola shape. I sometimes wonder if she knows what clothes that fit like hers do to the mind state of a young boy. As we walk in Miss Mims stops what she is doing and looks at both of us, pointing with her long nails. "You two go into my office, I need to talk with you." Once we make it into the office Ms. Mims begins, "Let me begin by saying, I want to hear both sides of your views about what has transpired between the two of you. I am going to listen to both of you and you each will have the opportunity to tell your side of the story. But what we are not going to do is talk while the other person is talking. That being said, Marvin you start first." Marvin then started his side of the story. He first accused me of bumping into him intentionally. He then stated, "Man, he didn't apologize, and then on top of that, started talking stuff, so I handled my business. He pushed me first and I hit him." I then just shook my head. I couldn't believe how he just lied on me. He also stated that when he saw me at the skating ring, I walked in and told all my boys to get him. He also stated that I and a group of boys jumped him. After that he had the nerve to say, I came to school and attacked him again. If you listen to his side of the story, you would think I was America's Most Notorious Gangster, instead of a scared kid who got beat down. Miss. Mims listened to his side of the story then I began my story. I stated that I did bump into him, but that I did not do it on purpose. I admitted that I did not apologize, because he pushed me and threatened me, before I had the chance. I then told her about how he continued to punch me until my eye was swollen. I told her about, how at the party, I didn't even know a fight was about to start until my friends saw him and they attacked him and his friends. I told her I didn't have anything to do with the fight. As far as today, I admitted that I had saw him and his boys in the cafeteria and tried to leave to avoid them. I told her how I couldn't run once we made it to Mr. Willis's class, since they were directly in front of the room. I told Miss. Mims that I decided to grab Marvin because I didn't want him to start punching me, like he did last time. Miss. Mims then looked at both of us and stated, "I think that this conflict is something that started over miscommunication and neither of you, being willing to back down. The question I have for you is; do you think it was worth it? But one thing I would like to know is how do you think we can resolve this conflict?" Both of us looked at each other in a defiant manner, but then I thought, someone has got to be the bigger person. "I first would like to apologize for bumping into you Marvin, I feel like we should let it go. I mean you beat me up and some of the boys in my apartment complex jumped you. Both of us are already in trouble and about to be suspended. I think we should just let it go." Marvin looked at me with a look like its not over, but played the role anyway. "I agree with Lewis, I think this was a dumb conflict that we should just let go. Next time I am going to just walk away. Marvin then looked at me sarcastically and stated, "Please accept my apology for punching you." As Marvin was speaking, we heard a knock at the door. "Hello," Miss. Mims, I came by because I am acting as Lewis's mentor, and I just phoned to ask his mother, can I act as his mentor." So once you finish with these gentlemen, could you please send them to my class?" Miss Mims looked over at Mr. Willis with her beautiful smile and stated, "Sure, Mr. Willis, I should be finished with these gentlemen in a few moments."

Chapter Eleven

WILLIS ASSIGNMENT

Miss. Mims gave us a pass to Mr. Willis and I knew we were in for a lecture and all types of punishments. I would much rather deal with the principal than deal with Mr. Willis. See Mr. Willis knows how to say things that just make you feel so bad. As we walked to the room, all I could think was how I would have much rather dealt with the principal. As we walked Marvin continued to give me the evil eye. I can tell, he really felt like this is not over. He then stated, under his breath, as we walked, "Don't think that this is over. I got you when I catch you at the skate night." Little did he know, when Momma finds out about this fight, If I am still alive, I definitely want get a chance to go to skate night again or anywhere else. I looked at Marvin and shaking my head in desperation, "Look man, I just want to let it go." When we made it to Mr. Willis's room he is sitting at his desk. He greets us, stating angrily, with a frown of disappointment on his face, "You two young men take a seat. I need to talk some sense into you." Mr. Willis had a thick vanilla folder sitting on his desk. Since we were slow to sit down, Mr. Willis gazed at both of us, this time a little nicer sitting but still with the same look of disappointment, "Take a seat gentlemen, I have something I want to share with you." We watched Mr. Willis nervously, anticipating what it is he has to share. Mr. Willis then reached into this thick vanilla folder. He takes out news clippings, mug shots and obituaries. Mr. Willis then looks at both of us and stated, "Do you see these men? I taught them." Mr. Willis then grabs another folder and places it on the table, next to the other folder. He then pulled out a few news clippings, pictures and graduation programs. Mr. Willis looked at both us and stated, "You see these are some of the students who I have taught over the years. What do you notice about this group, as opposed to this group?" Marvin and I just looked. I knew Marvin wouldn't answer, so I decided to. "On this side, these students finished high school and college and are in the paper for accomplishments. On this side, your former students are in the paper under obituaries or for crimes. And all of these students have prison pictures." Mr. Willis then stated, "Thank You. What you do now, determines what you are going to become tomorrow. This is the age of accountability where you guys decide what direction you are going to go in life." My question to you is, "What direction are you going to take?" We both paused and then look at each other shame faced. Mr. Willis looked at both of us, "Don't act shy now, look at the pictures and tell me which one of these paths you want to take?" Marvin and I walked around for a moment from group to group. "I then stopped and picked up a picture of a boy who had been charged with murder at the age of seventeen. Mr. Willis noticed me gazing at the mug shots and stated, "I see you have Michael's profile, Michael was really not a bad child. I taught him in the seventh grade. Michael was smart and could have been a talented athlete. He was a good basketball player and football player and don't mention baseball. But Michael decided he wanted to start hanging with the boys in his project home. Michael stopped coming to school regularly and began hanging out with a group of friends going the wrong way. His mother was on drugs and his grandmother was doing her best to raise him. But, instead of going to school Michael would rather hangout by the carwash and try to commit crime. Michael ended up dropping out. He then joined a gang and ended up committing a robbery in a stolen car with some older guys. Michael was sixteen at the time and one of the boys, well; the other boy was eighteen at the time. The other child received life and Michael was given twenty-years." Mr. Willis paused, I guess to let us digest the story then stated, "The reason I shared all this information with you is I want you to know that this is the age where you start to make a lot of your own decisions. And these critical decisions will decide which direction you are going to take your lives." Mr. Willis then asked us, "So which direction do you gentlemen want to go?" Both of us looked at Mr. Willis embarrassed and told him that we want to go in the right direction. Mr. Willis then looked at us and stated, "That's good, now we have the right mind state. Here is what I want to do. I want to mentor both of you and enroll you in this program, me and some of my fraternity brothers have developed. You must first get approval from your parents. Also, I want you gentlemen to do me favor, research a person who has been successful in whatever it is you want to do with your life. Write two pages on what that person did to accomplish his goals starting from your age. If there are no questions, you gentlemen may go." Mr. Willis then hands us forms, our parents need to sign for us to enroll in the program. I don't know about Marvin, but those pictures really made me think, I don't want to end up in jail and I really want to be successful and make momma proud. It's just when you are a young boy, you don't always think about what you do and how the decisions you make now, can impact your future. It's hard when you are trying to be a boy, as well as a man, and don't have anybody around to show you how to be a man. Daddy, I know he loves us but, I can remember the look in his eyes when momma would say we needed stuff and he couldn't afford it. Every time it made him feel like less of a man. I was young, but I can still remember that defeated look in his eyes. Sometimes Daddy would be almost in tears. I remember him saying to Momma, "A man isn't a man, if he can't provide for his seeds."

Chapter Twelve

VISITING DADDY

I can smell bacon and hear the popping sound of the bacon in the pan on Saturday and Sunday mornings. Even though we can sleep in on Saturday and Sunday, nothing is a better alarm than the smell of momma's bacon and pancakes.

When Momma comes into the room, she instantly starts yanking the bed spread off the beds telling me and my brother to get up. Momma is rushing because she knows that if we don't hurry we are going to miss the bus down to Green Street the city prison to see Daddy. See if we don't get in on time, even if we are a minute late, we don't get to see Daddy. This is a lot better than when he was in the southern part of the state. We only saw him once then when Uncle Ray took us to see him for Thanksgiving when I was eight.

Grandma is going to meet us on the 13, it's about thirty minutes away. In order to see Daddy we have to get up at 6:00 a.m in the morning. We then have to be out of the house by 7:30 a.m to catch the bus. That's a difficult task when Momma has Alisha to get ready and cook breakfast. I help her out by getting me and Brian ready. I am so excited about seeing Daddy; I just shake off my sleepiness. Momma has to iron.

By the time, me and Brian walks in for breakfast, momma and Alisha are standing up from the table. Momma hands me and Brian a sandwich and some juice and rushes us towards the door. Some of the people at momma's job think Momma is weird because of her energy. Momma walks with a long stride and has a tendency to get excited and sometimes talks kind of loud. Momma was raised in the South, so she talks a little country, but she is definitely not dumb. Momma is from the old school, so she doesn't believe in wasting anything. Momma always told us about how it was when she was growing up, chopping cotton from sun up to sun down. Momma can tell you anything you want to know about politics or history. She reads constantly even though she didn't go to college or anything like that.

Crawford Lee Penitentiary is not the type of place you want to piss off the security guards. Some families come in cursing, crying and acting crazy, why I don't know. The security guards are just doing their job, but some of them can be nasty. The problem with arguing with the guards is they have the power to deny you the right to see the prisoner you came to see or move you down to the bottom of the list.

But Grandma, being the hard-head she is, started cursing under her breath and fussing out loud. Grandma knows what could happen, but grandma is a drinker. Daddy said she has been drinking like that all her life; it's a family tradition on Grandma's side of the family. Daddy said that's why he doesn't drink period because of what he experienced growing up with Grandma's drinking. The grim faced correctional officer looked at Grandma and us with slightly red eyes. I can see the look on his sleepy face as he looks at Grandma and then down at us. I can tell his facial expression and gestures change when he looks at us. The officer decided to ignore Grandma for the sake of us kids. After about thirty minutes, we make it into the waiting room. Even after making it into the waiting room, we still have to wait fifteen minutes for them to bring Daddy.

The minute Daddy sees us he instantly begins to smile. Momma looks at Daddy always with tears in her eyes. Daddy then states, "I got good news for you." The government started this new program to assist prisoners. I am getting my GED. Also, I am learning a trade, I am learning carpentry and heating and air conditioning." Daddy actually looked happy for a change. Momma didn't ruin it for him by letting him know about my recent troubles. I kind of got the cue from Momma and didn't mention it when Daddy asked me how I had been doing in school.

Chapter Thirteen

"TRIP TO THE OTHER SIDE"

I didn't know what to write about the assignment Mr. Willis gave us. For most of the weekend, I didn't even think about doing the assignment. For some reason, it stayed on my mind. So to keep Momma off my case, as well as Mr. Willis, I decided to just write without even thinking about it. The essay went like this:

When I grow up or become an adult, I can't say I know what I want to be. I know all my short life, I have been feeling like I and everyone else is born for a purpose. I guess the purpose comes from outside of us, probably from God. I know I want to do something to make the world better. I probably would like to be a lawyer, but I don't know for sure. I know I want to make my family proud.

My purpose in life is to do something to make lives better for the people in the struggle. I read a lot so I know that it is not good for a lot of black people all over the world but also a lot of other people. I want to study hard so every child on this earth can have an opportunity to eat well, have a decent place to live and be happy. Today too many people get cheated out of happiness because the people blessed with the money want do anything with it to help those that don't have. I want to make my Momma proud and buy her a house. I want my sisters and brothers to be able to look up to me. I don't want to be a J or in and out of jail, that's for sure. I want to have a beautiful life like on T.V. The families on T.V always go on vacation, and there is always plenty to eat. I don't want to constantly worry about how to pay the gas bill, or the lights being turned off. I want to be able to give my kids everything they need. I want to be someone my son can look up to. I guess to get this, you got to have plenty of money, and it seems like lawyers make good money.

Also, people respect lawyers, and they help people. My father's lawyer has pictures with celebrities and big time politicians. But he still cares about the people from the hood. My father's lawyer told Momma he is going to help Daddy get out of jail. When I grow up, I want to help people. Just because a person makes one mistake, that doesn't mean he is not a good person. I want to be able to give people a second chance.

When we got to school, I didn't know what Mr. Willis was going to think about my essay. I walked in early. Mr. Willis was writing information on the board, with his back was turned as his gospel music played softly. "Good morning, Mr. Willis." I stated to get his attention. Mr. Willis turned around kind of shocked. "How is it going, you are here kind of early?" I looked at Mr. Willis nervously and stated, "I was just coming by to bring the essay you asked me to write." I then took out the essay. Mr. Willis stated,

"Well go ahead son, I am listening." I looked at him kind of surprised; I was thinking I would just leave the essay with him. I should have known Mr. Willis wouldn't make it that easy. Mr. Willis then turned with a semi-smile and stated, "Put it in the atmosphere, I am waiting to hear it." I paused and began to read the essay. As I read, Mr. Willis just stood their listening, like he always does. After I finished, Mr. Willis just cracked a smile again and then stated, "Meet me at 4:00. I will call your Mother and see if I can drop you off from school."

When I made it to Mr. Willis's room, Marvin was waiting along with Mr. Willis. Mr. Willis gave both of us a poem and asked us to read the poem. After reading the poem Mr. Willis asked us what we thought about the poem. Me and Marvin looked at each other, neither one of us knew really what to say. Mr. Willis then stated, "The poem I asked you to read was written by Robert Frost. It's an important poem at this stage of life. I know you have some opinion." I was like forget it, I might as well say something, if I don't Mr. Willis will never let us out of here. "I think the poem is saying, we all have choices in the direction we want to take our lives. We can go the wrong way or right way, and that is what decides our destiny." Mr. Willis just looked at me as always and nodded his head with a blank expression. Then he asked, "And what is your opinion, Marvin?" Marvin looked around as if the classroom was full, and Mr. Willis was talking to another student. Then he stated, "I agree with Marvin, also I think, it was kind of saying most people choose the wrong road, but it's that very few that choose the right way, that end up making it out of the forest."

Mr. Willis then stated, "Alright, well if that is the case, what is the forest?" Marvin then stated, "I think the forest is a lot of things: like the hood, jail, drugs, and all the other things that keep people down and stop them from rising." Mr. Willis responded, "Good view, I tell you what. Let's take a ride; I want to introduce you to some people."

We then followed Mr. Willis and got into his little gold Honda Accord. Mr. Willis drove us downtown as we listened to Jazz. We then drove up to this real, nice building and parked.

We entered the building and walked to the front. An older man dressed in a burgundy suit about fifty or sixty smiled and stated, "Good evening Sir, and who will you be visiting today?" Mr. Willis replied, "I am here to see," Mr. McMullen. The bell hop then phoned Mr. McMullen's office and confirmed our appointment. Then he said," Right this way, I'll take you up to Mr. McMullen's office. As we went up, Marvin whispered to me, "Whoever this Mr. Mc Mullen man is, he sure is paid that's no doubt." Once we made it into Mr. McMullen's office he greeted us with a smile. "What's up brother, are these the young men you have been talking to me about, come on in?" Mr. Willis and Mr. McMullen then shook hands, given their secret handshake. The office was amazing. Everything was expensive or looked expensive for that matter. Hand painted pictures were on the wall of famous African-Americans like: Thurgood Marshall, Martin Luther King, W.E.B. Dubois and other people I didn't know. Mr. McMullen looked at us and stated, "Would you boys like a soda or something?" Mr. McMullen then hit a buzzer, "Meghan, could you please bring two sodas for the boys that just came in." Mr. McMullen then punched another button which caused a LCD to turn down to the middle of the conference table in his office. Mr. McMullen stated, "I hear one of you wants to be a lawyer, and the other one of you gentlemen wants to be a music artist." Mr. Willis then stated, "Yes, both of these young men have a lot of potential. They just need someone to point them in the right direction." Mr. Lawson looked at Mr. Willis smiling with confidence, and stated, "I think me and Tim definitely will be able to help these gentlemen." Mr. McMullen then flipped on the screen and stated, "GC, are we ready to start to conference?" Me and Marvin instantly looked like we were about to faint, when we saw none other than GC. I mean I didn't want to seem like a groupie or anything so I tried to stay cool. GC then stated, "What's up, little brothers." I noticed he was dressed a lot different than he does on his videos. He had on a pink Ralph Lauren Polo shirt and slacks with brown shiny loafers. You could see the loud colors of the argon socks. I didn't expect this from a rapper from one of the worst neighborhoods in the city. Even though, GC's arms were filled with tattoos, he still looked like a regular business man that probably went to college or something. This was a total contradiction to the jeans, t-shirt and chains; We see him wear on the videos. Mr. McMullen then looked over at us smiling and stated, "These are some new brothers, we are going to induct into the mentoring program." GC then stated," I hope these brothers are real because you know I am serious." Mr. Willis then interjected," I am confident they will do the right thing." GC then shook his head and stated," Well it's all good, I look forward to meeting them. I am on my way to Miami, so I will holler when I get back." Mr. Lawson began explaining the program to us. He told us how he started the program. When he was a young boy, he used to get in trouble. Mr. Lawson told us how he was a good student, but he lacked guidance. He said he would always get in fights and was going down the wrong path. His grandmother took him to this church for vacation Bible school, and they had a mentoring program. He told us that a group of men in the church had started this mentoring program, and his mother wanted him to join. That was when he met this remarkable man named Dr. Simpson. Dr. Simpson was a Professor at a prestigious black college. He told us that Dr. Simpson took him under his wing, even though he had two sons of his own. He treated him like a son. As a result he was exposed to things; he wouldn't have seen and just started changing. He said that he promised Dr. Simpson he would pass it forward. Even though he is successful, he places a lot of emphasis on the mentoring program, more than anything in his life, besides God and his family. Mr. Lawson showed us a picture of Dr. Simpson hanging on his wall, a distinguished looking bald guy, with a bow tie and pinstriped suit. He discussed how important education was, and why his success is not about him. One thing Mr. Lawson said that stuck with me was, "You don't get an education just for yourself. You get an education, so that you can do something to help others, and contribute to making the world a better place. Every person is born for a reason, and has some higher calling on their life, and so do you, young men."

That night all I could do was think about those words. Just going to that law office, changed my whole outlook on life. Where I am from, you don't see black men like Mr. Willis or Mr. Lawson, all I see is black men broken down.

In the hood, all the men got baby momma's and stay with women. Most men sale drugs, pimp, or work jobs that don't pay much. When you are growing up, and that's all you see, it sometimes makes you feel like your destiny is their reality. But when you meet somebody like Mr. Lawson telling you that he came from the same hood, and he had the same situation and made it. This makes you think I can do it to. That night I dreamed my new reality. I dreamed that I was grown, had finished law school, and had my own law firm. In the dream, I was married to Tiffany, and we had two children, a girl and a boy. I had just gotten off work and was pulling into my nice garage, and gotten out of my Mercedes Benz. As I opened the door, Tiffany greeted me with a smile and open arms. She had on this elegant dress and a pearl necklace like the women on T.V. Before she could hug me, my kids ran and hugged me. She shook her head smiling, as I smiled back. Next thing I know the alarm rang. I was back to my reality, my world. But my world didn't seem like my prison any more because now I could see the benefits of choosing to take the other path.

Chapter Fourteen

KAREEM MORE DRAMA ANOTHER FIGHT

No matter what you may dream, the sad reality is, you always got to wake up. Some people have nightmares and wake up to a good reality. Some people dream their fantasies and wake up to their night mares, I guess that's me. No matter what my dreams told me my future will be, I still have to pass through the nightmare of the reality I live in now. Nothing like another boring day in Math class, even though Ms. Marshall tries to make class interesting, math is just boring to me. I do pretty well in the class compared to other years in math, but sometimes it's hard to focus especially with Tiffany sitting in front of me. The teacher brought me back into reality quickly. Ms. Marshall was standing in front of me smiling, but clearly angry. "Lewis, I know you are not sitting in class day dreaming again, if you can't pay attention now, you can pay attention after school. I need you focused now, take number three." I know I am in trouble because all I have been doing is day dreaming so I can't possibly answer this question. Ms. Marshall is an excellent teacher, kind of jolly, like Santa Clause. Ms. Marshall may be stern, but you can tell she cares about us learning. You can tell when she is mad because her eyes seemed to pierce over her glasses, as she gazes at you, kind of like she is doing me, at this moment. I start to attempt to answer the question, and all of a sudden Tiffany raises her hand. Ms. Marshall, I thought you said, we were going to do a group challenge on today."

Ms. Marshall then tells us to get into our groups. Two students in our group are absent, and one person in two other groups is absent also. So Ms. Marshall tells me and the person in my group to sit with another group. Tiffany's group happens to be one of the groups, and Tiffany smiles and motions me to join her group. In her group are Kareem and Tamika. Kareem and Tamika kind of eye me, as I take a seat in their group. I know what they are thinking, why didn't Tiffany choose Matthew? Even though I am a pretty good student in all my classes, Math is the one subject I do have problems in. Matthew, on the other hand, is a "brainy kid," especially in Math. Everyone knows that at the end of the challenge Ms. Marshall gives out those big snickers to the group that wins the challenge. Before I can sit down, Kareem and Tamika begin to question Tiffany's choice. Kareem states with a disappointed look, "Man, Why did you pick him, you know Matthew can answer every question." As Tamika shook her head in agreement, she pouted. Tamika then looked at me rolling her eyes, as she blurts out to Ms. Marshall, "I don't want to play anymore, can I just watch?" Ms. Marshall walked towards our group smiling and stated,

"Tamika, working with others, is a part of life that you will face throughout life in school, the community, and work. You might as well get accustomed to working with people, and situations you don't like." Tamika just listened, as she rolled her eyes in defiance, looking towards me to indicate her unhappiness with her new group member.

Ms. Marshall began the challenge. Each group is given a ticket to answer their question and a board to write down how they got their answer. Ms. Marshall set the timer on the memo board and gives each group sixty seconds to answer the question on the memo board. The first question was not that difficult, it was a word problem, and we all were able to figure out this question. Kareem busily wrote the formula for completing the question. We got that one right and were actually able to get the last seven questions write. As we entered the eighth question, our group was presently tied with Matthew's group, of course. When Ms. Marshall posted the eighth question, I knew then we were in trouble. This problem involved an algebra expression, we had just started learning. To add to the problem, I really didn't understand the problem. Kareem and Tamika instantly started to get nervous. Kareem began to pout, "See man, I told you not to pick him, now we are about to lose." Tiffany continued to write the formula, as I looked embarrassed, and Tamika and Kareem continued to complain. Luckily, Tiffany was able to answer this question. So as we entered the last two rounds, we were still tied with Matthews's group. When Ms. Marshall posted the ninth question, I knew we were in trouble. I am not good at decimals, and I knew the two complainers, probably didn't know the answer either. So here we were depending on Tiffany, again. We all looked at the problem, as the time ticked away. I decided to write the formula down. Tiffany asked me to move the decimal, but just as I started to, Ms. Marshall asked us to hold up the boards. Instantly, the room got quiet. Then Ms. Marshall surveyed the answers and the formulas. When she made it to our group Ms. Marshall paused, "Group three, I see that you chose the correct answer, but you have the decimals in incorrect spots so that disqualifies your group." Instantly Kareem and Tamika looked at me like they wanted me to just drop dead. Kareem then stated, "I told you not to pick this lame. I knew we were going to lose." After the game, Kareem continued to talk about me under his breath, "We should have known Lewis wouldn't be able to add a decimal. Broke as he looks, he never had the chance to count money." I had gotten tired of his mouth, so finally I spoke up. "Look man, I been trying to ignore you, but you keep talking, just leave me along." All of a sudden Kareem pushed me in the face with his hand, "Do something then, fool." I instantly looked at him, embarrassed and just jumped up, "Man, why you hit me?" Next thing I know, Kareem punches me and slams me to the ground. He then starts punching me as Ms. Marshall asked the students to go and grab Mr. Greene. Still on the ground, Kareem began to kick me constantly.

Chapter Fifteen

LET MOMMA DOWN AGAIN

I ts messed up when you get beat up, and you get suspended. But that's the way it goes at Garvey Middle School. I feel like I just can't get anything right these days. Momma was so disappointed; she couldn't even look at me. They gave me three days at home. The principal thinks I am some kind of trouble maker, and Momma doesn't know what to do. Last night I heard her crying, as she was talking to her friend, Cheryl. Momma said, she had missed the deadline to file for her food stamps, so now she couldn't sell any food stamps to pay the light bill. Momma said she didn't know what she was going to do, and then she had to worry about my mess. Cheryl is Momma's best friend or only friend, for that matter. Cheryl used to be on drugs real bad, but now she is no longer on drugs. She also has HIV, but Momma doesn't know I know. It's funny how adults try to talk in code, like kids can't understand. But Ms. Cheryl does not let it get her down, she is always happy and she takes good care of her kids, when they are with her. They live with Ms. Cheryl's, older sister. They live in the suburbs; she has two daughters, fifteen and seventeen.

Tonight I couldn't sleep, because of the guilt, how could I let Momma down like this? But I also feel like everybody is against me. I don't fit in there, anyway. School is somewhere for perfect people, if you think about it. People that look good, got nice clothes, and are real smart. It's a good place for people that know how to make other people feel like they are nothing. Everybody else, like me, are just coming to school for the amusement of the popular kids. I can't help how I look or what clothes I wear. That whole night, I just stayed up tossing and turning, trying to understand why I couldn't be the kid with the good looks and nice clothes. If I was that person I wouldn't joke people, I would treat everybody right.

The next morning, Momma woke me up, bright and early. "Lewis wake up, don't think you are going to sit in this house all day and do nothing." Momma stood over me with her scarf around her head, surveying my sloppy room. "Look at how you got stuff all over this floor." Momma stated as she pointed angrily. "The first thing I want you to do is clean this room, and here is a list of the other chores you need to finish before I get off work, and you also need to finish the school work, your teachers gave you."

Chapter Sixteen

SUSPENSION PARTY

Momma must have given me the longest list she could come up with. Momma wants to make sure I don't have any opportunity to enjoy my suspension. Momma looked at me in an angry way, and stated, "When I get home this house better be spic and span. And all your school work better be done, that's the first thing I am going to check." She then grabbed her purse and hurried out of the room, ushering my sister and brother to come with her as the bus pulled up.

I immediately got up and started working on the list. Momma wants me to clean out the tub. Make up her bed and our beds. She also wanted me to hang up all the clothes and clean under our beds. The next thing I had to do was scrub the walls. I first decided to scrub the bathroom. All of a sudden, I hear a knock at the door. It is Jason and Robert. I looked through the door and debated whether to answer. I am cool with Jason, but I know, whenever Jason is around Robert he is going to be up to something. Jason continues to knock as if they know that I am in the house. I know I didn't tell them about me getting suspended, but they had to find out from somewhere. Jason yells, "Man open up the door this me, Jason." I hesitated for a minute and decided to open the door. I know Momma told me not to have anybody in the house. When I opened the door, Jason instantly begins smiling along with Robert, aka trouble. "What's up, man, I heard you got suspended for three days, what are you getting into today?" Then he gestured his hand for me to give him dap. Robert followed Jason's gesture of friendship, as they walked in uninvited. "Man, I am just chilling, but my Momma is tripping. I got all these chores, plus I have my school work to do." Jason then stated, "Man, we skipping today. We got these girls we met. I ought to call them over and see what they talking about." Now I know what Momma told me about no company, but I don't want to make myself look lame, so I didn't know what to say. I then looked at him, unsure and stated, "Man, I don't know about that, man my Momma been tripping, I don't want to get in anymore trouble." Jason then put his hand on my shoulder and stated, "Man don't worry about that, your Momma doesn't have a car, and she all the way on the other side of town, at work. How is she going to find out?" Robert, then of course, had to put his two cents in, "Yeah man, stop being scary, you know it's all good." Jason followed his usual routine and jumped on my computer. Jason and Robert proceeded to get on face book while I went back to finishing my chores. The whole time I am cleaning, I am thinking Jason is sure changing since he went to alternative school. I guess being around all those bad boys making him change. I know it was already around him because of his big brothers, but I see something different in Jason. He acts like he doesn't care about skipping school hanging with people who are up to no good. But I don't want to say anything to Jason because that's the only friend I got. As I continued to clean, Jason's phone began to ring. I could hear him state to the person on the phone, "What's up Felecia, what are you up to?" as he slapped Roberts hand, with a devilish smile. He then stated, "I'm just hanging out over my boy L house, what are you and your girls up to?" Whatever Felecia was saying on the other end must have been good because Jason's eyes continued to light up as they talked, and he smiled at me and Robert. "Yeah it's all good. You and your girls can come by, my boy Lewis's Mom is at work," Jason answered without even thinking to ask me if it was ok. Once he got off the phone, I lit into him, "Man why did you invite those girls to my house, knowing that my Momma told me I couldn't have any company. It's bad enough that I got you two over here." Jason then shook his head, "Lewis, its all good, man your Mom don't even have a car, how is she going to catch you, she all the way across town at work." Jason could tell by the look in my eyes that I was not feeling any of the stuff he was saying. He then added, "Come on, man, look out for your boy." I knew that Jason was basically saying man look out for me, how I look out for you. I then hesitated and stated, "Man, they can come by, but they can only stay for a little while."

Jason and Robert went down to the beginning of the apartment complex to meet the girls. I knew the girls had to be wild if they were skipping school. Jason said they were girls from the west side. Jason knocked on the door, and then walked in with Robert and the three girls following behind him. Jason then introduced us, "This is my boy L and this is Felecia, he stated smiling at Felecia, as he looked her up and down, and these are her girls Tee-Tee and Keisha. Felicia was dark and had pretty eyes, she also looked fully grown. Felecia looked and dressed like a grown woman. I knew that was what made Jason want to talk to her. She has on tight pants which only showed off her thick thighs. She could easily have gone for a freshman in college. Her friends Keisha and Tee-Tee were obviously the followers. Tee-Tee was kind of short and had Chinese looking eyes. Keisha was actually kind of good looking, she has mild skin, which complements her brown eyes, and is skinny and kind of tall. But you could tell by her face, that she had a bad attitude. Felicia then stated, "What's up man, I thought we were coming over here to have some fun, it is lame as hell over here." Tee-Tee and Keisha then laughed and join in, "I know we didn't just come over here to look, play some music or something. Where is the food?" Jason then stated, "Man Robert, go grab them something to eat from the store." I knew Robert didn't have any money. That meant he was going down to the corner store to steal something to eat for the girls. Robert looked at him and then stated, "Oh, it's all good I got it as long as Tee-Tee coming with me." Felicia then looked over at Tee-Tee, "Gone go with him girl, I'm hungry." Tee looked at Felicia with a smirk and then rolled her eyes at Robert, "I'll go, but don't think that mean I like you shorty." Robert then jumped up with his pants hanging off his backside proceeding for the door with Tee-Tee. Before Robert could even close the door well, Jason was on the prowl. "Felicia, why you so mean, he stated," as he slapped at Felicia's face. Felicia then smiled as she pretended to chase Jason to get her lick back. Jason ducked into my room.

This was just all part of his plan to get Felecia along so he could feel on her and kiss her. Of course, Felicia knew this, and continued to smile as she fell into the trap. While those two continued from the front room to the back room, I was stuck keeping Keisha company. Even though I was nervous and I knew Keisha would not dare talk to me, plus she had a bad attitude, I still tried to be nice to her. "You want to watch something on T.V?" I asked as I continued to pretend to clean. "No, I'm good she stated." Then all of a sudden, Keisha pulled out a lighter and a brown cigar, stuffed with marijuana. Even though I didn't smoke, you can't grow up in my hood and not know a blunt when you see one. Keisha glanced over at me, just before she got ready to light up the blunt. "My bad, you want to smoke with me?" I looked over at Keisha thinking she must be crazy, not only do I not want to smoke with her, but I don't even want this stuff in my house. "No, I'm good; you can't smoke that in here, either." Keisha looked at me shaking her head, "Man why the hell did we come over here, if you tripping like this shorty?" Keisha jumped up walking towards the room were Felecia and Jason were, "Man lets go," she stated angrily," These dudes are lame, you can't even smoke in here." Jason then looked over at me, L chill man; it's all good; it's just a little blunt. Robert got some spray you can spray, your mom want know nothing." Jason then looked back at Keisha, go ahead and light it up, Keisha then lit the blunt and inhaled. She then passed it to Felicia, who also inhaled, smiling as she moved closer to Jason. What I saw next, I couldn't believe, Felicia passed the blunt to Jason. Jason grabbed the blunt and inhaled as if he had been smoking for years. J then passed it to me, expecting me to hit the blunt. I was already in shock from seeing him smoking weed. I looked at Jason as if he was someone I had never seen before. As he inhaled the smoke, it seemed like his eyes just got tight and he had this weird evil look on his face. I then looked at Jason and stated, "Man you got to be crazy, if you think I am going to smoke some dope. Man I thought you were better than that." All of a sudden, I heard a knock at the door. I ran to the door and almost fainted. Ms. Cheryl was at the door. As she knocked I could see her looking as if she could see through the door. Ms. Cheryl must have seen all the traffic coming up to the apartment and got suspicious. I looked at Jason and the rest of those fools, "See what you got me into now, my momma's friend is out there and it smells just like weed." Keisha then stated, "Deuces I am about to go. I will holler at you guys later." he stated with a nonchalant don't care attitude as he pulled up his pants. I then stated, "No you are not." pushing him back from the door, clearly angry, I need all of you to go into my room until Ms. Cheryl leaves." I then cracked the door, "Hey, how are you doing Ms. Cheryl?" Ms. Cheryl looked at me clearly suspicious as her eyes gazed the front room as she attempted to look around me she stated, "I was just coming by, your momma told me you were suspended and she ask me to come by and check on you." I then stated with a nervous look trying to look comfortable, "I am doing well, I am just doing the chores Momma asked me to do, and then I am going to start on my homework." Ms. Cheryl then started to inch in between the door crack as she started to sniff she stated, "What's that smell, Lewis?" as she walked through the door. Instantly I knew I was dead. Ms. Cheryl walked in, all everyone could do was pause in shock, as one of the girls tried to hide the marijuana behind her back. As Ms. Cheryl walked towards me, everyone instantly went scrambling for the door. Ms. Cheryl then looked at me, "Lewis, now you know better than this, here it is your Momma already going through enough, and you in her house doing drugs." I couldn't do anything but hang my head. Ms. Cheryl then stated as she shook her head, "Boy, don't you know, you playing with death. Drugs will take you somewhere you don't want to be. Yeah, I hear you kids joke about junkies on the street and stuff but you don't know." Ms. Cheryl stated as she looked like she was about to go into tears as she choked. "You don't know how it feels to want to stop doing something that you know is bad for you and that messes up everything in your life, but you can't stop. It's like you need it, like you need air to breath and nothing else matters. I started out messing with marijuana when I was your age. Look how I ended up. I destroyed my life, battling with drugs." I listened to Ms. Cheryl for over thirty minutes, only mumbling, yes, with my head bent every few minutes. Even though I knew I didn't do the drugs, I figured why try to tell Ms. Cheryl that? I figured it would be better to show remorse and hope I could get her to pity me enough not to tell Momma. Ms. Cheryl doesn't like drugs because she was addicted to crack cocaine for years and it caused her children to be taken.

Chapter Seventeen

MR. WILLIS PROGRAM

Today we went to orientation Mr. Willis picked me and Marvin up at the school. He drove us down to the University for the Orientation. Mr. McGinnis came up to speak. Their were about fifty kids from all over the city. We sat in an old meeting room waiting for the guest speaker to come up as people passed out water and snacks.

I and Marvin took a seat next to Mr. Willis who introduced us to Mr. Wilson who had four young men with him. "Good evening Mr. Wilson these are two brothers that are new to the program, this will be their first year. Mr. Wilson then stated, "It is a pleasure to meet you these are some young men that enrolled in the program on last year this is Terrell, Jarvis, Zavier and Toby." All of the boys looked happy smiling from ear to ear, to be here, how lame. How could you be happy being in a boring program?

A gray hair man then came to the front, "If I can get your attention we are ready to begin. If you will look several people are bringing in board games. But before you get to play the games I want to introduce those of you who are new to the program to someone, Walter Frye".

A midsized mild complexion man then came to the podium. "I want take a lot of your time but I will just say I look forward to teaching you chess this year. Chess is essential to understanding how to play the game of life. So as you play the games tonight do not hesitate to stop over in the chess session were I will have coaches available to get you acclimated to playing chess. That being said lets play games."

All over the room people were playing different board games. I have never played a board game in my life. Were I am from people play games like dice, spades or domino's. Me and Marvin were looking like are you serious. Mr. Willis then stated, "Let's play Monopoly hopefully we can win some tickets. I heard they have some interesting prizes tonight."

There were three people already playing the game as we approached. Mr. Willis looked at me and Marvin and then stated, "Don't worry I will walk you through the first game." As the dice rolled Mr. Willis then began to give us instructions. He explained that the theory of the game is to acquire property and wealth by using a strategy. Even though I lost I actually enjoyed the game.

By the end of the night we were called back to receive the prizes. Mr. Wilson came back to the front this time with a line of prizes as he smiled. The first two groups received gift certificates and everyone else received a ticket to the basketball game. Even though it started off lame I really enjoyed playing the games. It was a lot different than in my world were all you see is dice games which have been known to lead to fights and sometimes murders.

Chapter Eighteen

HOMELESS TRIP

E ven though it is Saturday, I am waking up early like I have to go to school or something. Today we are going downtown to feed the homeless. We spent all yesterday getting together our clothes. We had a clothing drive where we gathered clothing for lots of people in the community, churches and stores participated. Mr. Willis and I and a couple of other guys went around picking up the clothes. We used Mr. Wilson's van. Mr. Wilson owns an electronics shop on South Street. Mr. Wilson had his son Kevin to drive us around to pick up the clothes. It was actually kind of fun; we stop at the Pizza King which is owned by Mr. Smith, he made us a pizza and some wings. He even let us go to the back and we watched as he demonstrated how pizza is made. A nice beautiful looking high school girl was in the back making the pizza. Melissa looked at us and smiled as she walked me through the process of making a pizza. I had to get up early in the morning and catch the neighborhood bus down the street. Momma had already talked to Ms. Reed and she agreed to drop me off at the school. This helped at least I didn't have to get up an hour earlier to catch the bus. As we drove to the school I had to endure listening to another one of Ms. Reed's lectures about young people. If I have to listen to one more of Ms. Reeds speeches about rap music, sagging pants, and fast girls, I promise you I am going to cut myself. When we make it to the school, there are ten other people waiting in front of the school. Mr. Willis pulled up in the bus shortly, and we stopped at three more schools along the way. Once we made it to downtown, we parked at a vacant lot next to a bus station and an abandoned building.

Mr. Murphy, one of the mentors then gave us our directions and warnings about how to deal with the homeless. "Please do not get rude with the homeless even if they are rude with you. Some of the homeless are sick and have mental illnesses. "Mr. Murphy then assigned each person their duties. I was placed in the drinks area. We then began setting up the clothing station. Each type of clothing was divided up and a person was assigned to give one piece of clothing to each person who wanted an item. The meal consisted of cakes, fish, chicken, mixed vegetables, corn bread and greens, peas and potatoes. Me and Marvin along with a kid name Carlos was assigned the drink area. All we did was pour the tea and juice and pass it out to the homeless as they went down the line. All of a sudden a bus with the picture of the famous rappers Will C rolled and Big Mike. Out of the van jumped Will C's momma and several other people. They came out with bags holding toothbrush, tooth paste, soap, sanitizer, and socks. Next, the bus rode up with the members of the band and chorus. They then began to set up. Within minutes of getting everything set up the homeless started to invade the area. Marvin stated, "Man they just came out of nowhere, like they can smell that chicken." As we served the people that came up, I as well as the other students were in disbelief. I mean, here it is I thought I had it bad. These people didn't have clean clothes or a way to bath. One man walked up who looked like he was about fifty or sixty. You could smell him a mile away. He had gray hair and was just a little taller than me. The man all of a sudden took out his teeth right in front of everyone. The saliva and nastiness of it would have ruined any person's appetite. But the homeless people just kept going through the line as if what he had done was not gross. After a moment the chorus began playing music. The homeless then began to sit around the parking lot mostly on the stumps reserved for parking and ate mostly quietly as they listened to the music. A couple of families actually came up with children with them. This made me even more thankful; here it is, I am always thinking about how bad I got it since I have to wear hand me down clothes. These kids have bigger problems; they don't even know where their next meal is coming from, nor have a place to stay.

After we had served the food, a lot of the homeless sat around listening to the music, three men even started dancing. The men danced side by side, each one competing with the other to impress the growing crowd. As people began to cheer the men continued to dance. Everyone seemed to enjoy the dancing after a while the saxophone player began to dance with the men as more people crowded around to watch. It is amazing how people, who have so little, can find a way to be happy despite their circumstances.

Chapter Nineteen

THE HOSPICE

When we entered the hospice, we were greeted by this nice white woman that looked like she was about grandma's age. We were all taken to a room where we were seated and two women and a man came in. The nice woman greeted us and told us her name was Ms. Williams, Ms. Williams then introduced us to three other people, "These are three special people, who would like to speak to you on today before you tour the hospice." The first woman stood up, a young looking woman slightly overweight. "Good morning, everyone, my name is Shirley Evans and I and my friends would like to speak with you today for just a brief moment," the woman stated as she smiled and looked around the crowd as if she was trying to look each person in their eyes. As she spoke someone had started to pass note cards and pencils through the crowd. "If you will look, all of you should have received a note card and a pencil so that you can write down questions you may have. Allow me to introduce my two friends in the struggle, Yvonne Simmons and Roderick Green." Both of the people smiled and kind of waved as she introduced them. They both looked like they were happy to be speaking this morning. All that was going through my head was I will be so happy when they finish the presentation so we can go to the Hawks game.

Shirley began first, "Good evening everyone, my name is Shirley Evans and I am HIV positive. Now when you look at me, I know what you are thinking. She doesn't look like she is HIV positive. She doesn't look like she has AIDs but please understand I do. Before me and my friends speak with you about the dangers of HIV/AIDS I want you to watch a video about a very special person who this facility happens to be named after, Monica Lewis. Monica died from complications related to HIV/AIDS at twenty seven years of age. Monica had dealt with HIV/AIDS since the age of fifteen and she spent her entire life making teens and young adults aware of the dangers of HIV/AIDS. Today I want to show you a film Monica created, a couple of weeks prior to her death."

On the picture outside in the lobby Monica looked real good. She had a nice shape and had beautiful black hair, a caramel colored face, and a beautiful smile. But on the video she was skin to the bones and you could see sores all over her face. As she coughed she began to speak straining for words.

I chose to do this video, in my condition, because I wanted to get your attention. I want people to see the actual end of the fight against HIV/AIDS. I contracted HIV when I was fifteen years old. At that time I was just entering high school. I had become real rebellious. My momma would try to tell me to slow down, but I wouldn't listen. I would go to the skating ring with my friends and a lot of times come home past curfew.

One particular night, I met this older guy; he must have been about seventeen. He was nice looking and he asked me if I wanted a ride home. I knew that Momma was expecting me at home, but I just had to get in the car. We rode around for a few moments. I was just happy to be riding around in the city, seeing the lights and listening to the music. We talked, and then we went to the Burger Hut and ate. After a while, I told him I had to go home. We stopped outside, down the street from my house. My heart was beating and my palms were sweating. For the first time in my life, I felt like I was in love. But I did not know at the time that love would cost me my life. See when you are young; sometimes you don't think you allow your emotions to guide your decisions. Well anyway, he kissed me and said goodnight. That kiss that lasted ten seconds seemed like it lasted forever. That night when I got home I didn't care about getting in trouble, all that was on my mind was Ricky, and I felt like I was in love.

Even while I was on punishment I tried every chance I could to contact Ricky. Little did I know that why I wasn't around, Ricky was seeing other girls throughout the city. Finally I got off punishment, and Ricky asked me to meet him at a store after school, and that was the beginning of the end. Well I made decisions that a child should not make, until they are ready. A decision I knew could cause me to possibly have a child, that I could not care for, or cause me to contract a disease which could possibly ruin my life or even end my life.

I continued to sneak around being grown. One day Ricky came to me. I was so excited to see him; I didn't know what to do. But today he looked sad. He looked sadder than I ever saw a person look. I could see a fear I had never seen, as he cried, he came to me with a paper and the worst news I ever heard. He said he had found out he had HIV. I didn't know what to say I just started crying.

After that for a long time, I just walked around the blocks from my home crying. Finally I went to a church down the street with tears in my eyes. Scared, afraid to breathe, all I could think of was what am I going to do. What am I going to tell Momma?

After a while I walked in the house. Momma was in the house along with grandmother and my older sister and little brother. When I walked in, I just busted out crying. I told Momma why I was crying and she and grandmother just started crying, as they held me.

Momma took me to the hospital, and they ran test, as we waited on the results. When we went to the hospital, I was just praying that just maybe I wouldn't have it. Momma and I sat and waited and finally they called me in. They ran some test and sure enough I had HIV. When we went home that night, my whole family cried the entire night. It was like I had died. I don't know if it hurt them worse than it hurt me. I remember thinking it would have been better if no one had known I had the disease.

From that moment on, I became a changed person. Some people would have given up if they were going through what I was going through. But because of my family, church, and counselors I kept going to school. I even went to college and completed a degree in community counseling. For many years, I lived in fear of people finding out I had HIV. Once

I became a counselor, I gained the confidence to start to tell my story in awareness programs.

I noticed that when I was healthy and I told people my story, they didn't recognize the seriousness of contracting HIV/AIDS. So I began to ask HIV/AIDS patients in the last stages of the disease to share their AIDS story or As I Die Slowly story, as we like to call it. I would then show a picture of the patient in the final stages of the disease.

But this video is for awareness, as well as a special person in my life. You see during the course of that short relationship which changed my life, a miracle occurred. Not only did I contract HIV, I also became pregnant. Luckily I conceived a child who through blessings does not have HIV.

So, I would like to take this time to let you see me and my pain (As I die slowly). To my precious child, Miracle, and children of the world, don't be in a rush to make decisions which can destroy your opportunity at pursuing your destiny and happiness. My testimony of what I have endured the feelings of shame, embarrassment, and fear, the physical pain of the disease now, and the lost opportunity to see my child grow up. If me, showing you and Miracle how the disease affected my life helps you to make the right decision, then maybe my life was not in vain. It's a beautiful world out here if you ever learn how to live in it. This involves making the right decisions when choices of life present themselves. I am begging you, please make the right choice because you see what happens if you don't make the right decision.

When the video ended you could hear a pin drop in the room. Most kids heads were down, eyes were watery, and I was doing all I could not to cry. The speaker's must have been used to this sort of response because they just paused for a minute and allowed us to digest the video.

That night all I could do was think about how the woman's body looked. As I tried to sleep, all I kept seeing was Monica Lewis. How could a beautiful woman have been inflicted with this disease? The thought of seeing her with sores and so skinny you could see her bones were an image that I knew I would never forget. However, I knew that no matter what, I didn't want to be that way.

Chapter Twenty

THE FESTIVAL

Today Mr. Willis informed us that we were invited to a fest at the East End community center. The community center is in the middle of the Eastside between four projects. The community center is the all purpose building for the community it is used for everything from weddings, funerals, parties to meetings. When we rode up to the community center you could see old buildings all around some vacant some occupied. The light brown building had jumpers and several booths set up outside. We were volunteered to chaperon by the Program.

The program is a celebration that is held year to recognize graduates of the outreach program. The program every year has a guest speaker who speaks to the youth about his life on and now off drugs. All around the carnival you could see kids playing. In one area they were having a cake walk. Women from the church bake their cake receipts and each person walks around to the music to see if they would land on the number to win the cake. Another person was over the fish off were people could fish for a prize for one dollar. In the other booth boys were gathered around for the hoop contest. I was over the sack race. Ten contestants would pay to race to the finish line and the three winners received a prize. You could smell barbeque burgers and hotdogs in the air as everyone had a good time.

Finally Minster Rose walked up to the stage and stated as she paused to make sure the microphone worked properly, "Good evening everyone if I could get your attention. People then began to usher kids towards to stage and the events began to shut down as people moved to the stage. Mr. Rose stood patiently and then after a few moments stated, "I know many of you are having a good time but we wanted to take a few moments or so that we can introduce our key speaker for our graduates from the drug free course, none other than Samuel Jefferson." Mr. Jefferson walked to the podium with a smile as if he had just won the lottery. Mr. Jefferson then hugged Mr. Rose, as he walked off the stage.

Mr. Jefferson then paused for a moment as his facial expression changed from a smile to a very serious look as he glanced at the crowd. He then stated, "Hello my name is Samuel Jefferson and I am a drug addict. Now I may not look like a drug addict now but please believe I am one. I was born in the heart of the East side the Mound. All of my life I was a gifted athlete from little league baseball to park football I was always a star. I quickly gained a name for my ability to run the football and throw a baseball. In the hood when you are successful athlete everybody looks up to you and wants you around. My entire life I was always treated special. When I went to the store people in the neighborhood would shake my hand and all of the hustlers and drug dealers were always giving me money and praise.

By the time I made to high school I must have been about tenth grade I went to a party. I had just run for over 150 yards and we had beaten our city rival. When I came in the party it was like was a movie star. Everyone's eyes were on me as everybody walked up praising me and shaking my hand. Finally, a couple of seniors from the team asked me to come in the room. When I went in the room all the guys were passing joints around. Larry the star receiver passed the joint to me and kind of coached me into hitting the joint. You know how people do when they are trying to convince you to do something they have never done we call it coaching. Anyway I smoked the joint and it became my new best friend. The minute I smoked marijuana it seemed like we were getting high after practice and sometimes after and before school. The crazy part about it is I still did well in football and no one even knew I was high every day except my closest friends. I graduated high school and received a full scholarship to State University one of the top football programs in the country, and one of the top party schools also.

My first semester it was a slight culture shock, first of all in college there were different kids from different back grounds, races, nationalities and incomes. With these differences also bought different drugs. My first year felt like it went by in one week. From the moment I entered the University it was as if we went into the league. I was given a brand new car and I had access to money whenever I needed. All I had to do was do was what I do best run the football. My freshman year I ran for nine hundred yards. Instantly, I was the future of the University and who is who on campus and I was high every day. You name it from every kind of pill legal to illegal plus my old friend Mary Jane. The first year was one big party.

By my sophomores year I was so popular that when I went to class people asked for my autograph. I was going to classes, practice, film viewings and then study hall. Directly, after that I was getting high. It seemed like every other week I was trying a different pill. Despite my drug usage I started the year off with a bang, breaking the State single game rushing record. By game two I was the man but something tragic happened during that game. I tore my ACL after that everything went downhill. I stayed out the rest of the season as my leg healed after the surgery. When the doctors cleared me to play I was so excited the first game everyone was anticipating me coming back. I ran the ball the first play and everyone cheered as I gained six yards. On the next play I ran the ball and was tackled on a blitz as I tried to go out of bounds I felt a sharp pain as the player from the other team tackled me. I just yelled out as I held my leg with my head bent down in the ground. It's a day I will never forget because on that day everything that mattered died even though I was not dead physically, but it's the day all my dreams and vision died. All that was going through my head is what am I going to do now? How am I going to buy Momma a house?

After the surgery my career was over. I still had my scholarship and I could have finished school. But after the leg injury everything changed. I was now becoming a normal student. It is difficult not to be treated like a king when that's all you have known every since you picked up a football.

But I saw that I was still respected on the party scene. The fraternity boys were all too eager to invite me to their parties and give me all I could drink and all the drugs I could do as they talked about my success prior to the injury. I would just listen after a few months because football was no longer my life drugs were. After a while I stopped going to class and started just getting high. Of course this caused me to fail out of school. So at twenty one I had fallen from a potential first round draft pick to a college drop-out with a cocaine habit. After that I couldn't go home because I was ashamed.

Chapter Twenty-One

CAMPING TRIP

On today we are going a camping trip. This will be my first time leaving off of the Westside since we went to visit Daddy one Thanksgiving with Uncle Sederick. Even though camping seems kind of lame I did always wonder what it would be like to go camping when I would see it on TV. I used to watch movies with people camping never did I think I would get a chance to go camping. We all met up on early in the morning at Mr. Evans store in the parking lot.

The minute I got on the bus I fell asleep. When I woke up all I could see were trees. This was my first time going out of the city besides visiting Daddy in jail. To me this looked like another world. As I looked out of the window all I could see was land and trees. I let my window down I could not believe how clear the wind was. When we pulled into the park ground I could see a row of cabins. Once we made it to the camp grounds Mr. Wilson immediately stood up. You could tell people were excited because everyone was looking around and no one got quiet as he began to speak.

"Ok everyone let's get ready to unload. Once you unload line up near the bus so that we can go over a few ground rules." Once we got off the bus Mr. Wilson then began again. "Mr. Williams is about to pass each person a name card with a number. Based on you card number this will decide who you will team with on the trip. Each group will have five young men and two adults in each group. You will need to stay with the people in your group at all times. First we will all hike to the camping grounds. You will first be given your camping gear and your back packs. Many of you have never been camping so we will first begin teaching you how to construct your tents. Next we will all meet up to go fishing and then we will prepare and eat lunch. Next, we will complete the obstacle contest. After this we will then complete the arts project. Once we have finished the art project we will then go canoeing. After canoeing we will then have our cook-off and lastly our ghost stories. Keep in mind each team will receive points from one to five. After the completion the winner will receive the Empowerment Camping Competition trophies. Also, each group member will receive a 100 dollar gift certificate from Nike.

I was placed in group blue. In my group Mrs. Frye and Mr. Mason are acting as our camp guides. Mr. Frye and Mr. Mason stood in the corner as Mr. Mason waved the blue flag. As we walked up Mr. Frye began to hand each of us blue t-shirts with Empowerment program written on the shirts of course. Mr. Frye then stated, "Blue teams are you ready for an excellent camping experience. I want you to feel like you are a person back in the days when we didn't have all this technology. I want you to see how man can survive without the computer, iPod, television, heat and all the other things you think you need." He then looked around at each of us like a captain in the military and then stated, "How many of you have been in the Boy Scouts?" One of the boys then stated, "I have I was a Boy Scout for three years." Mr. Frye then replied, "Do you know how to construct a tent son?" Then boy then stated, "Yes Sir." Mr. Frye then stated, "Then come up to the front to assist me in demonstrating to the other students how to construct a tent."

I should have known Roderick would be the one to raise his hand. Since we have been in the program he has always been the know it all. Roderick is a book worm. He is always reading and attends the magnet school for math and science. Roderick instantly came up with his tent in hand. Roderick then stated, sounding like a teacher, "Everyone grab your tents. Then open your tent and sit each piece out. After this take the inner tent and lay it out like a blanket." We all began to lay the tent out as he instructed. Mr. Frye and Mr. Mason then began to assist us as Roderick waited for us to finish this task. He then stated, "Take your stakes and push a stake down in each hold at the edge of your inner tent." We then begin placing the stakes down. That only took five minutes. Roderick then held up a long metal piece in his hand and stated, "Next, these are tent poles. Watch as I snap my poles together. Know I am placing the pole into the holes at the edge of the inner tent. Lastly I am placing the poles into the hole at the edge of the tent." As he placed the poles into the tent the tent quickly transformed from a blanket on the ground to a full tent. We instantly began to follow his instructions and in less than minutes our tents were up also. We all were happy as Brian even attempted to go into his tent. Mr. Mason then stated as he smiled admiring the excitement the tent demonstration had created, "We still have one more part to complete pay attention so Roderick can finish. Roderick then stated, "The last step is simple but you may need to help each other." Mr. Mason then came forward and he and Roderick grabbed the outer tent. He then observed the outer tent to make sure it was placed properly. Roderick then grabbed four pegs and secured the outer tent completing the tent. Roderick then stated, "An bang just like that you have completed your tent." We instantly began following Roderick's instructions. Marvin assisted me and I assisted him in completing our tents. We all then went into our tents. "Man this is alright; I could get me a tent and move out of my Momma's house." Marvin stated as he admired his new found home.

"Ok, gentlemen lets go ahead and pack our tents back up neatly. Make sure you have each piece. We are now ready for the fishing contest. Each of you will receive a fishing pole. We will first add string to our fishing poles. Next, you will place the bait on the hooks and spread out. Each fish you catch will be placed in the blue bucket. Alright blue team follow me we are about to began to hike to the lake to fish."

When we made it to the fishing pond Mr. Cummings was waiting with a big smile and a referee suit. As the teams all made it to the lake Mr. Cummings blew the whistle. And then stated, "You will have two hours to fish each group member will place the fish from his group in the bucket. At the end I will count the fish and award five points to the person with the most, the runner up will receive four, the second runner up will receive tree and so fourth. Good luck".

As I cast my first reel I then began to fish. As the people in my group fished I looked around at how peaceful everything was. "Please watch the ball when the ball starts to move or go down alert me and then start to pull your pole up.", Mr. Frye stated. As we fished it didn't take long before someone from the yellow team across the lake yelled, "I got one." Next, a member of the blue team caught a fish and the red team. As we continued to fish the teams continued to catch fish except our team. Freddie then stated, "We are the only group not catching fish. The people in this group don't know how to fish." After a few moments the time referee came up. "You have thirty minutes left good luck groups." As the last thirty minutes began to end we finally caught our first fish. Freddie of all people caught the first fish. A few moments later I saw the ball began to move on my fish. Then the ball instantly began to go down as I yanked the pole forward. I then yelled I got one, Mr. Mason then ran over and helped me to pull the fish in. Mr. Mason held the fish up on the line and stated, "We may not do well in the competition but if it was based on weight of fish I think we would have won this competition." Once the fish were counted up the gold team lead with six fish, the red team had four fish, my team the blue team caught three and the purple team finished last with two fish.

Next we hiked over to the other side of the lake. We were welcomed by a college student, a tan skinned white boy with long hair that looked like a young college student. Hello, campers I hope you are enjoying your camping experience. My name is Wild Fire and I am a Choctaw Indian Are you ready to learn how to canoe?" We all looked at the man with little enthusiasm and stated, "Yeah." I know most people were at least curious like me but no one is going to make himself look lame by showing too much enthusiasm. Wild fire first showed us how to enter a canoe. Afterwards he demonstrated how we should hold the paddle. He then began to show us how to paddle. As he showed us each step he made us do it and watched and corrected our mistakes. After about thirty minutes we began to practice how to canoe individually. Mr. Mason placed us in groups and we were ready to begin the canoeing contest.

As the whistle blew Mr. Cummings stood up, "We will begin the canoe contest in approximately ten minutes. You can now gather your groups and head to the start line, he stated. Mr. Mason then stated, "Lewis you will sit in the rear left with Marvin and Roderick and Brian will race take the front. Remember if you begin as a team you will end as a team. Marvin you will do the count, remember 123 pull." We then began paddling towards the start line. "Line your canoes up on the line. When you hear the sound of the whistle you may begin whoever makes it to the end line and back first will be declared the winner and the points will be awarded accordingly to the other three groups", Mr. Cummings stated. As we entered the start line we grabbed our paddles and held them as Wildfire had showed us.

Mr. Cummings then blew the whistle. Marvin then stated, "1, 2,3 pull." We then began to pull the other groups began without a count and started out ahead of us. Marvin continued to follow the instructions and yelled again, "123". As Marvin yelled we continued to follow his instructions. Eventually the red group began to stall. As we passed them we then rolled continued to follow Marvin's count as we turned the turn line. Marvin then paused as we braced ourselves to return. He then yelled the count again by the second count we made it to the yellow team and we passed them. We then continued until we made it to the purple team. When they saw us come one of the purple team yelled. "Hurry up man they are coming up on us." We continued to move to the count as we move towards the purple team. After two counts we passed them. As we pulled to the finish line Mr. Mason and Mr. Frye were waiting with a smile on their faces. As we got out of the canoe the other groups were still attempting to finish the race. "I told you work as a team and you will win finish on top. Teamwork that's what it is all about", Mr. Mason stated. The purple team came in second, the yellow third and the red team last.

We then hiked back to the camping grounds to begin the cooking competition. "We are now about to discuss how we will be cooking. We want to win the contest for our group so I decided that we are going to do chopped smoke turkey and grilled Italian sausage with my father's signature barbeque sauce. Also, Mr. Frye will assist you in making grilled vegetables. Lewis and Marvin first grab the grill stack the grill with charcoal and place them in a pyramid. Roderick and Brian assist Mr. Frye in preparing the vegetables." As we prepared the grill Roderick and Brian placed meat and vegetables on sticks and wrapped corn to be placed on the grill. "Now I am about to light the grill. We will wait for the fire to die down and the coals to turn gray". Mr. Mason stated as he pulled out a long lighter and lit the grill instantly fire shot up and smoke shift to the sky. Once the coals were down the meat was placed on the grill. As I smelled the barbeque cooking I couldn't wait to sample some of the barbeque. In the other camping groups you could smell the aroma of fresh cooked food as well. I could tell that at least one group was grilling like us.

After an hour we heard the whistle blow as Mr. Cummings called each group to move to the middle of the camp grounds for the cooking competition. Each group came up with the meals they prepared and placed them on the judges table.

The purple group presented their food first they prepared shrimp and steak shish kebabs. They also prepared grill asparagus wrapped in bacon. The red team prepared tin foil stew. The yellow team prepared chicken breast and camp fire potatoes. The judges walked around to sample the food. Finally Mr. Cummings blew the whistle. He then stated, "As it relates to the cooking contest we have a problem. Each group did so well that we came to a decision. As it relates to the cooking contest we will rule this a tie. This means that each group will receive four points for this competition. So now you are free to move from group to group and eat as you please. Once we finish eating you will break back into groups so that we may prepare for the ghost story contest."

After the cooking contest we received our story line. The story line comprised of a four page mock story which we need to brainstorm as a group to complete the story. We all were placed in our groups for an hour to decide on a story. As we began to contemplate a story line, Marvin stated, "Man I don't know what we are going to do. We could have won the championship, but there is no way we are going to come up with a story to win this competition." I then stated, "Man I think I have a idea. There is a story my Daddy tells my sister and brother to teach them to tell the truth. It is called Mr. Boo." Brian and Marvin instantly began laughing as Brian yelled out, "BOO". He then stated, "We are not creating a comedy story we are creating a ghost story." As they laughed

Mr. Frye then stated, "At least allow him to explain his story to you? And Marvin and Brian you can't criticize his idea if you don't have an alternative idea." Roderick then chimed in, "That's true lets at least listen to the story of Mr. Boo."

After all the jokes I really didn't want to tell the story but I went ahead anyway. "Once upon a time there was a girl named Mary. Mary loved to tell fibs, lie or trick people whichever you choose to call it. Her parents would always warn her about being truthful but Mary would not listen because she loved to lie. Her brother and sister would often get angry with her for tricking them or deceiving them. One night as Mary was sleeping safely in her bed she heard a sound coming from her window. "Boo, Boo, My name is Mr. BOO!", the ghost stated, "I came to get you and take you away for lying." The girl began to cry and plead as she yelled, "Please Mr. Boo don't take me away I want lie again! Mr. Boo looked at the girl and yelled I don't believe you. Then he grabbed her and took her to the deep dark woods far away. The girl then began to plead and cry but Mr. Boo didn't care. Her family woke up crying when they saw Mary was gone. Mary's family all mourned and cried as they looked for their daughter. Finally her brother found a letter it said.

Dear Family,

I came to get Mary because she told too many lies. To all the boys and girls let this be a lesson to you; tell the truth or Mr. BOO will come and take you to the woods far away where you can't tell lies to anyone.

Once I finished the story Marvin then stated, "It's a straight story but it just sounds like a ghost story for a little child. But still we will roll with it." Roderick then stated as he looked at the template, "I think if we change it up a little to fit the template this story should work."

Shortly afterwards Mr. Cummings blew the whistle to begin the competition. We all sat under a campfire as each group told their story. After the other groups told their story I got up to tell our story since I know the story best. At the end of the story everyone was laughing but I think that they enjoyed the story. Mr. Cummings then stated, "We have now concluded the contest and the winner is the red team and the runner-up is blue team. Even though we didn't win the contest we came in as runner up.

Even though we didn't win I enjoyed us competing as a team. By the end of the trip I felt like we were not just blue team for the trip but a team for real. It's amazing how me and Marvin were enemies but now we are working together as a team.

Chapter Twenty-Two

THE TRIP

Today we are leaving for our Civil Rights trip. But this is not just a trip this is a five state tour of black historical sites were speakers will be there to meet us. I couldn't sleep last night I was so excited. I was just happy to get out of the city. Before joining the program the furthest I had been was South Georgia to visit Daddy when he was in jail. We began the trip going to Martin Luther King Jr.'s monument down town. We then went on a tour of Ebenezer Church. Everywhere we went we took pictures, all of us were dressed in our black shirts with gold letters. The front of the shirt read "The Empowerment Program". We just call it the program. Dr. Watkins calls it the program.

After we finished at Ebenezer Church we head to the historic Atlanta University Center. There we visited Clark Atlanta University, Morehouse College, Morris Brown College and Spellman College. We then went to dinner at the famous Pachal's restaurant. After that we loaded up to head to Montgomery, Alabama. Once we made it twenty minutes outside of the bus Mr. Rollins stood up, I need everyone's attention," he stated as he paused waiting for everyone to follow his directions he then preceded. I have something I want you to watch. Mr. Rollins then turned on a documentary. In the documentary we saw Dr. Martin Luther King and several men crossing over a bridge. As they crossed over the bridge you could hear them singing and see them smiling, happy to be fighting the good fight, on the right side of history. As they crossed the bridge all of a sudden a mob appear converging upon them. The mob was lead by police officers waving bully clubs with German Sheppard dogs. We watched as the mob began to unmercifully beat the marchers. We watched as dogs bit the marchers and the people as they cringed and covered their heads. Everyone in the bus was quiet. As I stared at the film I felt both anger and pain. How could one person be so cruel towards other people just because of their color? As we parked Mr. Rollins then stood up, "I hope you see why it is so important for you take education serious. These men and women you saw on this film and many were beaten, berated, jailed and some even killed to give you the equality you have today. This is why you have equal access to education and opportunity today. So young people always remember you owe someone for the rights you have today. So you owe it to these people to be good stewards of the opportunities bestowed upon you. This involves take advantage of the opportunities you have to advance yourself and be an asset to your community as well as people all over the world. Every person on this bus was born with a purpose. It's up to you to find out what that purpose is and fulfill your destiny. These are just some of the people whom fought for you to have the right to pursue your destiny with equality. Now we are going to participate in a mock march across the bridge. As we March across this bridge we will be singing a song. The black national anthem, "We Shall Over Come." To those of you who don't know the song please pick up the lyrics as you exit the bus."

As we walked out of the bus there were other people waiting for us. I was shocked to see people white, black and Mexican all waiting to march across the bridge with us. As we marched across the bridge we all began to sing, "We Shall Over Come". As I walked and we sang it seemed as if I could was in a time capsule. I actually felt like I was one of the Civil Rights activist. As we neared the bridge's ending I could see Mr. Rollins and the other men marching with their heads up with pride. When we made it to the end of the bridge police officers were waiting. For a moment I started to think maybe the officers are about to do the same thing the officers did back on bloody Tuesday. Instead the officers were waiting and began to sing along with us as we boarded the bus. The officers then lead us down the path sirens blowing in front of us until we made it to our next stop Alabama State University. Once we made it to Alabama State we were met by a group of men from Mr. William's fraternity. The men were dressed in black suits with black and gold ties. I was impressed with how shiny their shoes were. They took us on a tour and then at the end of the tour we were taken to the auditorium. I couldn't believe it Peoples himself was in the auditorium. A person is one of the hottest rappers out. As we walked in Peoples stopped his speech. "Come in young brothers and sisters. I was just talking to the seniors in the music department you can join in this conversation too", Peoples stated as he paused and waited for us to take a seat. "When you see me on the television rapping that's just one aspect of what I do. A few years ago I was a student here just like you. Even then I was working hard. I was a member of the band, the vice president of my fraternity and maintained a 3.5 G.PA as a business major. While I was not consumed with these responsibilities I was rapping. I remember plenty of nights staying up until the next morning with other aspiring rappers working on our dreams of becoming big time rappers. But one thing I didn't do was allow my dreams to stop me from working towards my goal. My goal was to be an entrepreneur. I knew if I studied hard and learned about business I could accomplish this goal.

But my dream was something I could not guarantee, but I needed it to give my life meaning. So I never stopped rapping or dreaming. But I also never stopped working towards my goal. Let me show you the benefit of this decision. Not only did I become a successful musician. I also became a more successful entrepreneur. The education I gained in college better prepared me to manage the wealth I accumulated from my dream. That's why I have been able to start a clothing line, purchase a store with a major franchise, as well as, other investments I have undertaken. So when I look at myself I consider myself not a rapper but a businessman who one of his businesses happens to be rap. While my dream may have been to be a rapper, look at all of the successful rappers who have lasting careers in the industry. They are constantly marketing themselves and changing their marketing strategy as the audiences preferences change. They are diversifying their capital and investing in new businesses. This is important because it is guys like this that give money back to the college's so that other students will have the opportunities to grow and develop new ideas and opportunities to make lives better for other students. That is why I am here with the honor to be in the position to donate this check. This money will be used to fund a studio and provide business courses specifically designed for students interested in pursuing a music career. Lastly, always remember you cannot go forward if you don't give back."

The crowd instantly began to cheer as the music began to ground out the crowd. Peoples then began to yell, "When I say Alabama" you say State" the crowd then yelled "State" as he ended stating, "Aaaaaa Mmmm." You would have never expected Peoples to be a college campus. And to see how intelligent he spoke really surprised me. I thought Peoples was just a regular hood dude. Peoples really inspired me. He showed me that rap and the music industry is still just another business. It seems like the person who understands business is going to make the money. It is kind of like Mr. Roberts said its two types of people in economics buyers and sellers. The only person that is going to get rich is the person who is the seller.

Next we began our trip to Troy Universities Montgomery campus. Once we made it to the town we pulled in to the Rosa Parks museum. When we made it to the large museum I thought here we go another boring event. But when we made it to the inside of the museum we saw a space age museum with the past ready for us to relive. The tour guide first took us to a room to see a bus like the one Rosa Parks refused to get off of. The tour guide told us about how courageous Rosa Parks was. One woman who decided to take a stand sparked a movement which changed our live.

The most fascinating part of the tour was the time machine. This space age trip to Cleveland Avenue showed us how the voices of the pass paved the way for the opportunities we have in the future. As we took the trip back to the past I actually felt like I was back in the past. After this we went to the research room. Here we heard testimonies from people of the past who actually lived during the struggle for equality. As I went on this trip I knew that for the rest of my life I would always study hard to show these brave people that their struggles were not done in vain. I realized that the freedoms and opportunities we have to day came at a cost and I must work hard to pay the price for the opportunities which these heroic people gave me.

We spent the night in Montgomery and then began the long trip to the Mississippi Delta. This trip lead us to a remote area which took us back into the past even though it is the present. Many of the houses still looked like the films we had saw in classes as we passed to small towns in Tallachie County. As we rode into the town and turned down the street were the museum is located you could see five or six old building a few people were walking in and out of the old buildings that reminded me of ghost town establishments from old scary movies. The people were all very nice as they waved at us as we rode by.

The museum was not the type of museum you would see in the city. This museum was an old building which looked like an old warehouse. When we made it to the front door we viewed a video in which we heard an old man who was there when everything occurred with Emmitt. We heard his account of what happened. Next the tour guide took us to view artifacts from the incident and back in the days. He then took us and showed us a famous blues singer from the town. The most excited part of the exhibit was the replica casket and body of Emmitt Teal. When he showed us the replica it was hard to believe that a adult could do that to a kid just for trying to talk to a girl.

Chapter Twenty-Three

DADDY'S HOME

When I walked in the house, all I could smell was Grandmother's famous baked spaghetti and fresh corn bread. For some reason, momma seemed to glow today, like the sun in July. Daddy instantly began to smile when he saw me. I could tell he was kind of shocked at how big I had grown. I guess he couldn't really grasp how much I had grown up when we came to visit. I also felt kind of weird. It felt like my father was a different person like we had become strangers. I walked in and smiled back at Daddy with an awkward smile. It was different now from back when I was eight, just before Daddy got locked up. I would just run to him and hug him with no hesitation. But now I have grown older and it felt awkward hugging him. I think daddy felt the same way, but still moved towards me giving me a light hug as he wrapped his arms gently around my arms he stated, "How has it been going little man,? Your Momma told me you held it down."

Soon my sister and brother came home. They spent most of the night hanging off Daddy's lap. Cousins that we hadn't seen since daddy got locked up, all came by to visit. Most came with some kind of alcohol, as we played soul music throughout the night. People just sat around and ate and played spades and reminisced about old times. At least, that night it seemed like everyone forgot about all the day to day struggles associated with life. Uncle Al, my father's child hood friend's voice, could be heard above everyone. Uncle Al has a real, good sense of humor, and he loves to try to get people to laugh. He came over right after work; you could still see the oil on his shirt. Uncle Al always helps Daddy out when he has car trouble. They also like to barbeque and watch the football games. For a brief moment, we left this world of pain and not knowing. Finally, it felt like our super hero was back, the person who could make us a family. The person who gave us hope, which allowed us to dream, was home to make a house a home. Finally, the nightmare we had known without him was ending.

Chapter Twenty-Four

LOOKING FOR THE BETTER DAYS

I couldn't sleep for some reason and I woke up early this morning. I could hear daddy and momma talking in the other room. That's the thing about our small apartment, no matter how low you talk, people can pretty much hear your entire conversation. I could hear momma and daddy talking. Early in the morning is when they have their conversations about things they don't want us to hear about.

I could hear mother as she stated, "I told you Lewis, don't worry we are Ok. As long as I am getting enough hours, I can pay the bills and keep food on the table." Daddy stated, "I know you can pay the bills, but that is my job. I am a man, baby, I am not a peon, trying to live off of a woman." Momma then stated, "I know you are not a bum, but the economy is bad. You have got to be patient and give it some time." Daddy then stated, "I understand what you saying baby, but I did exactly what society said do. I made sure I learned a trade, so that when I get out, I can take care of you and the kids without doing anything illegal. But every time I apply for a job and they see the felony charge, I can't get a job." Momma then stated in a comforting manner, "Lewis, don't worry everything is going to work out." Daddy then stated, "Maurice wants to give me a job, working at his car wash and even offered to let me do some remodeling on his store." "Are you out of your mind? Lewis I love you to death, but I am telling you right now, if you take a job with Maurice, it's over. I don't care if we starve to death, I don't want you dealing with Maurice," momma stated!! Daddy then stated, "You don't know how it feels to be a man and have kids you can't take care of." Momma then stated, "Lewis I don't want to hear that. You don't know how it feels to raise three kids while their father and the man I love is behind bars. I love you, but I will leave you if you take a job with Maurice." I could hear the bed squeaking as Daddy got up as he angrily stated, "I am not going to take the job for now, but if I don't find any other options, I will and that's final."

Maurice was Daddy's friend since elementary school. Maurice Wilson is a local businessman/drug dealer. He and Daddy used to run together and he was the one who planned the incident that caused Daddy to go to prison. Momma felt like Maurice caused Daddy to get in trouble, so she doesn't want Daddy working for him. These days Maurice tries to portray himself as a businessman. He opened up a store, Real Estate Company and even opened a funeral home. Maurice now walks around with slacks and a polo shirt on and drives a fancy rich car. He even went back to college and earned a degree in business. Maurice gives out turkeys at his store for the homeless around Thanksgiving, but many people say he is still involved in drug selling.

I remember when Daddy had just been locked up; Maurice came by to try to give Momma some money. Momma took the money and threw it down the stairs. I can still remember the boys that were under the tree scrambling to try to pick up the money. After that Momma gave him some choice words and he never did show up again.

Chapter Twenty-Five

DRUGS FOR SALE

I got up this morning to get ready to walk to school. Jason always comes out when he has to walk to the bus stop to catch the bus to get to alternative school. Jason and Robert walked up both smiling as usual. "What's up L man check out my new shoes?" Jason and Robert both have on a new pair of the new Jordan's. I couldn't believe it. How could they afford those shoes? Jason then pulled out a large sum of money. Jason then pulled out a big roll of money. "Look man this is what I made last night." I couldn't believe it Jason has started selling drugs.

I just look thinking, how is it that I and my folks don't know how we are going to pay our bills or eat and they made that type of money in one night. The first thing that I started thinking was I wish I could jump in that game for a minute and make some money for the family real quick. But I knew Daddy would kill me if I got caught selling drugs. "Man I can't believe you are getting money like this. Man I want in." "No, Jason stated, if we let you in your Daddy is going to find out and you know this." Everyone knows that even though my Daddy is not in the street game anymore he still knows all the hustlers in the streets, and the first thing they would do if they saw me hanging on a corner is call him. Jason then looked at me and stated, "I tell you what I will give you something and let you work it. If that works out I will get you plugged in with my connection." I then looked at him happy as a man who just won the lottery and stated, "Man thanks J I want let you down."

We then walked down to end which is the corner on the outside of our apartment down the street from the corner store, wing shop and other little stores. River Street is a known drug trafficking street in the city. This means you have to be careful because someone can rob you and the narcotic agents are constantly in route. Once we made it to the corner Jason held out his hand with the bags and stated, "Look man here is ten bags sell these for ten and those for twenty. Stand over here next to the turn so you can get the business coming in. Don't worry about anyone robbing you because they already know what it is." I knew Jason was telling the truth about the fact that no one would try to rob. But who would protect me from the police and my father.

When the first person came up, he was tall and looked like the average J. His teeth were brown and decayed and he was dressed any kind of way with blood shot eyes. So this caused me not to hesitate to serve him. But he kept looking at me. Smiling as he shook his head and finger he stated, "Wait a minute little brother don't I know you. Yeah, I know you, you are Lewis little son I remember you when you were a baby what are you doing out here." I paused for a minute and then looked down the street at J and Larry. I could see that they were watching to see if I make the sale. I then looked at him and stated, "I am just out here trying to make a hustle." The man then stated, "I know you don't remember me but my name is Karl Jackson. I grew up on this block. When you were born I was a high school senior. I remember changing your diaper with your Daddy. I was a big time basketball player back then." I then looked at him and stated, "I remember you going to the league you got drafted to the Lifters." The man then smiled showing his brown teeth grinning from ear to ear stated, "That's right I am made it to the league but most people have forgot about that now." He then pulled out his money and took the bag. As he was about to leave he then turned around and looked at me seriously, "Little Lewis I know you probably aren't go listen cause I know I am nobody to be telling you this. But believe it or not I was a good basketball player. But before I got drafted I was dabbling on the streets trying to make a hustle. One day I was with my boys and someone talked me into trying cocaine and it has been downhill since. All of my talent went down the drain. Since I been out here in these streets I can tell you many days I wish I had made a different decision.

But I don't know which one is worse being a dope head like me or a hustler. I have been out here for years. You see the dope boys either getting locked down for long periods of time or getting killed every day and then another group comes to do the same thing. At the end everyone loses their children and everybody else that cares for them. But I am not going to preach to you, just make the right decision."

As he walked off J and Larry walked up. "I see you busted your cherry you in the game now." J stated as he shook my hand smiling. Larry stood back smiling nodding his head for approval as if anyone cared what he thought. As I looked at the man walking away I thought about what Daddy had said and Mr. Willis. Daddy told me about the sixty seconds rule In life you only have sixty seconds to make a decision and the choice you make will impact the rest of your life. Mr. Willis told me about the two roads. And then Daddy's friend Karl Jackson just confirmed it. I might be broke but I am not broken. Selling dope that's just something I can't do. I mean how can I sit up and get rich off someone else's misery. I grabbed the drugs out of my pocket and handed them over to J, "Man you all can have this. This is not me." I stated as I walked off.

Robert yelled out, "See Jason I told you he was lame. I don't know why you keep hanging around this dude." Jason then stated, "Man if he doesn't want to sell dope that doesn't make him lame, you lame and you sell drugs." I just continued to walk. I didn't look back because I didn't care what they had to say. When I made it home Daddy was waiting out on the porch. As I walked up I could see his eyes piercing from a distance. I could tell by his facial expression as I got closer he was angry about something. When I got closer it seemed like he was staring at me. All the time I am thinking I know I didn't get in trouble at school so what could it be? The minute I made it up the stairs I stated, "Hello Daddy is everything alright." Daddy then looks at me and stated, "Where were you at today?" I then looked at him already knowing where the conversation was going. Somebody had to tell him something. Daddy must have found out I was trying to sell drugs. I then looked at him sad and stated, "I was just hanging out for a few minutes with some of my friends." "Hanging with your friends? What did

I tell you to do? When school gets out come straight home."
I couldn't believe it here I was about to tell on myself and
he didn't e even know I had been on the block trying to sell
drugs.

Chapter Twenty-Six

DADDY'S RULES

I didn't know how to tell Mr. Willis I was out of the program. I didn't want to get out of the program, but Daddy said I had to leave the program. Daddy felt that the program was a waste of time, and that the men were trying to invade on his territory as a father. Daddy is from the old school, and some people think that when a man takes interest in a young man, he may be a molester or something. Daddy felt like the men in the program were not serious about helping black boys from the ghetto. He said they were just looking for a tax write off and a way to make them feel good about themselves. Daddy said most of the educated black people act like they are too good to come to the hood.

All day long I was trying to figure out what I was going to say. Finally, I came up with an idea. I will act out in Mr. Willis class. I will get in such a bad argument that he will be forced to kick me out the program. I tried to figure out what I could say to him to make him hate me. I know Mr. Willis takes education serious and hates when students interrupt him, so may be that was an option, but how could I make him angry. Mr. Willis is a calm person, he never shows emotion, so how can I get him to show some today.

I decided that first I would come to class late. Then when Mr. Willis asked me why I was late I would get smart with him. As the bell rang for my last class I went to the restroom and took a stall. This is where people go when they are planning to hide out to be late for class. I patiently waited until all the students had gone to class, even the people who are normally tardy just after the bell. I knew I had to be at least five minutes late for class at this moment. As I walked into the classroom I had already decided what I would say. I thought that Mr. Willis would say Lewis why are you late. I would then tell him man I am late because I wanted to be late for this boring class. I figured that the argument would start from that. I would then begin to ridicule his teaching and the program. I was hoping this would make him angry enough to turn his back on me. Then I could yell out that I wanted to quit his stupid program without him asking questions as to why.

When I walked into the class I intentionally opened the door loudly instantly diverting the classes' attention from Mr. Willis to me. Mr. Willis looked at me as I entered the class for a brief second and then stated, "Class, if you look at the diagram on the board you can better understand the problem Mexico faced." The students instantly diverted their attention back to me, as I took a seat wondering what I am going to do now that this didn't give me the opportunity to argue with Mr. Willis. I then came up with a brilliant solution. I would start making sounds as he taught. Mr. Willis then continued with the lesson and I began, Hmnn, Hmnn, Hmnn, Hmnn as loud as I could, once he turned his head. Mr. Willis then stopped and stated, "Whoever is humming could you please stop, as he look towards my direction. I then waited a few moments after he began and stated, "Hmnn, Hmnn, Hmnn." Mr. Willis immediately stopped class, "Lewis step outside the class for one moment." I walked out of the class as Mr. Willis followed and then stated, "Lewis, is everything ok, were you humming in class?" I then yelled at Mr. Willis loud enough for the class to hear, "I was humming to keep from going to sleep in your boring class." The students in the class instantly began to laugh and yell, "Ohh"!! Mr. Willis looked at me, shocked and obliviously disappointed, he stated, "Lewis, go sit in Mr. Greene's class and report to my room after school." I looked at Mr. Willis trying to conceal the shame I felt, as I walked off.

When I entered the class at the end of school, Mr. Willis was busily stacking books in a corner.

As I entered Mr. Willis class after school, I was still debating about whether to tell Mr. Willis the truth or not. As I sat down Mr. Willis then stated, "Lewis, what is going on, you are not acting like yourself, is there something you want to talk about?" I then tried to look mean as I stated, "Man it is nothing wrong with me, I am just tired of you and your stupid program." Mr. Willis then stated, "I thought you liked the program. Come on Lewis, tell me what's really happening." I then paused for a moment and then decided to tell the truth, "Mr. Willis I want to be in the program, but my father told me that I couldn't be in the program. He said the program didn't benefit me, and that men like you, don't really care about poor people."

Mr. Willis bucked his eyes as he heard my statement, as if he was shocked and then stated, "I hate that your father feels that way. I wonder, if I can call your father." I then stated, "I can give you the number, but I don't know if he will answer. He's been out looking for a job." Mr. Willis instantly grabbed his phone as I called out the numbers for him to dial. "Yes, is this Mr. Johnson? I was calling to speak with you about Lewis. "Mr. Willis then glanced back my way as he placed the phone down and stated, "Lewis you can go ahead and catch the late bus. I will talk to you on tomorrow."

When I got off the bus I could see Daddy standing on the porch waiting as I walked towards the house. The first thing I thought was, Daddy is going to be angry, thinking I asked Mr. Willis to call him. Instead, Daddy had a smile as I walked up and stated, "How was school today?" I looked at him kind of confused, knowing he just spoke to Mr. Willis and stated, "It was Ok." Dad then stated, "How was everything in Mr. Willis's class?" I then paused before stating, "I told him what you asked me to tell him." Daddy then looked at me knowing that Mr. Willis already told him everything. But instead stated, "I spoke with Mr. Willis and I think you should stay in this program. I was wrong about Mr. Willis, so I want you to stay in that program and listen to everything he is trying to teach you."

When I walked in the house I could hear momma on the phone, "Girl you are not going to believe this, but Lewis got a job." I looked around to see daddy smiling from ear to ear. "That's right, son, I got a job starting next Monday, thanks to you." I looked at him shocked, wondering what I did. Daddy then stated, "Mr. Willis called me on today, and we started talking about you. I explained to him my situation. When he found out that I was a licensed carpenter, he gave me the number to a contractor, and told me to use his name. The contractor hired me on the spot, no questions asked."

Chapter Twenty-Seven

LOVE LETTER

I hate it, today we are in the middle of class and I can't focus. All I can think about is Tiffany. I saw her in the hall today with her beautiful eyes and that cute smile. I just sat and watched. It is like, she is royalty, and everyone wants to give her a hug or just walk up to her. Leah and her click of course, don't feel that way. They are still angry at me for telling the principal about them tearing down those posters. I don't see why they were so angry, since Tiffany was going to win anyway. Even if they had not torn down the posters, Tiffany still would have won.

I finally made up my mind to tell Tiffany how I feel about her. But, who wouldn't love Tiffany? She is beautiful on the outside, but she is more beautiful on the inside. Tiffany brightens up every room she enters. Her smile and even the sound of her voice are beautiful. If only, I had the confidence to tell her how I feel. Since I couldn't say it to her, I decided to write it on paper.

Dear Tiffany,

I know that you don't know me that well. But I really want to get to know you better. I think you are the most beautiful girl at the school. Not just because you look good, but because you are good. You make everyone around you feel good. I wake up every day excited about school, rushing to get to school, so I can see your face and beautiful smile. And it's that same smile that I go to sleep with, sweet dreams thinking about. I wanted to tell you how I felt, but I get nervous when I am around you. I am glad I gave you this letter because, at least, I will be able to say I tried. I know if you were my girl, I would do all I could to make you the happiest girl in the world. You are my sunshine, my diamond, my everything!

I must have rewritten the letter about ten times. Even though the letter was short, I thought it did the job. It let Tiffany know that I really wanted to get to know her and was in love with her. I didn't want her to think I was a stalker or something. As I read the letter, I was so shy. I was afraid someone would look over my shoulder, and see what I was reading. I think the biggest fear I have, is rejection. I don't know what I would do if Tiffany rejected me. I have made up my mind, I am going to give the letter to Tiffany. I began to fold the letter up as the bell began to ring.

As I began to pick up my book bag, Leah pushed me and stated, "Get out of my way, ugly boy." As she walked by, she saw the letter in my hand and instantly snatched the letter out of my hand. I then ran up to her stating, "Give me my letter back." Leah handed the letter to her friend as she laughed, "Nicole, run girl." I looked at Leah like she had just committed murder, as my heart dropped. I could see a smirk of satisfaction on her face, as I ran out the room to chase Nicole. By the time I made it to the hall, Nicole had already run into the safe haven of the girl's restroom. Leah ran in shortly behind her. In less than two minutes I knew it was over. I could hear loud laughter outside of the girl's restroom, as they read the letter out loud.

As the girls walked out of the restroom I could hear them singing in unison, "Lewis and Tiffany sitting in the tree K-I-S-S-I-N-G". I could see a look of happiness on Leah's face as she sang with the rest of her friends. Leah walked up to me and stated, "Come on Lewis, I am going to take you to give this letter to Tiffany." I looked at her with shame and anger, as I snatched her hand back, "Can I have my letter back?" I stated pleading for sympathy. Nicole then stated, "Don't worry; I am going to tell Marcus, that he can stop dating Tiffany because, Lewis is stepping in." Nicole stated as she laughed devilishly.

Then to add fuel to the fire, Tiffany walked out of Mrs. Wiggin's room, and Leah and all her crew instantly ran to her. "I heard you have a new boyfriend. I guess I will let Marcus know about Lewis," Leah stated as she and her friends began laughing. Tiffany just stared at the girls, probably wondering what they were talking about. Nicole then handed her the letter. Tiffany took the letter and proceeded to read it. I felt like I was about to die. As Tiffany read the letter she looked at me, smiled, and walked off. When Tiffany walked off, the other girls continued to laugh and joke. One girl yelled, "Lewis wants to know your answer." At least, Tiffany had done me the favor of not embarrassing me in front of the entire school. I am convinced; it's that kind of embarrassment that makes people want to drop out of school.

To tell the truth, I was kind of relieved that Tiffany now knew how I felt. If that snake had not grabbed the letter, I know I probably wouldn't have been brave enough to give the letter to Tiffany. Another thing, at least Tiffany didn't reject me in front of the entire hall, like they were expecting.

Tiffany even turned her head, and it looked like she stared at me, once she got down the hall and kind of smiled. I was so embarrassed, and my heart was pumping like it was about to jump out of my shirt. I was in a trance, so I just sort of stood in the hall like a statue. I couldn't smile back because my face was frozen. Instead, some kind of way, I was able to remember how to walk, even in shock to a place I could hide out, the library.

Chapter Twenty-Eight

EACH ONE TEACH ONE WEEKEND

It is the each one, teaching one weekend? Today each person in the program is supposed to be matched up with a mentor who will help them in developing business skills. I was like I don't really know anything about business. Everybody in my family was just happy to find a job. In my neighborhood, the only businesses are liquor stores, corner stores, and hole in the wall clubs. The real business men are on the streets selling stuff, some legal and some illegal.

So when you say, black business, to tell the truth that is something new to me. When we made it to the each one, teach one room, we pulled up to this nice building on Campbell road. The building was new and looked nice, compared to most of the things in the area. When we entered the building, the first thing we saw was shiny floors, black and white. The long hall decorated with pictures from the past, all were pictures of smiling black men in nice suits. As we walked in, we were greeted by a man, who introduced himself as, Mr. Maxwell. Mr. Maxwell told us that he was Mr. Mathew Maxwell III and that his father was the founder of the Peoples Bank. I could not believe it, a black man actually owning a bank.

But that's not the end of it, the Distinguished Black Men of the city were there to represent. Every black business had a booth. We were all ushered in to take a seat as the presentation began. Mr. Maxwell, of course, started the night, "Good evening young men, it is my distinct pleasure to welcome you to the Distinguished Black Men, Each one, Teach one program. I know many of you know that African-Americans have made major accomplishments in entertainment and sports. Just in the chapter alone, the 100 Black Men have over seventy millionaires, with a combined net worth of close to 500 million dollars. Now I know you are thinking, what does that matter to me? Well, the 100 Black Men are not just men who are blessed but, we are men committed to fostering economic development in the black community, job creation, and most of all, preparing young people for entrepreneurship. Today, it is with great pleasure, that I introduce each of you, to a mentor who will seek to assist you in preparing for your futures, as young black entrepreneurs."

This is perhaps, of even more importance to me, since I am a leading founder of this program. But first, allow me to introduce you to the founder of the Each One, Teach One program, Founder, none other than, the honorable Mr. Willie Williams.

Mr. Williams walked up to the podium, as all the men stood up, smiling as they clapped and shook his hand.

Then, a tall grim faced man, who looked like he was close to a hundred, walked to the podium. He introduced himself, as Mr. Williams. Mr. Williams didn't look like the rest of the men. Mr. Williams was dressed in regular khakis and a button down shirt. He didn't have on a tie or a nice suit, like the other men, but they all seemed to respect him. He clearly didn't look like he fit in. Mr. Williams, then stated, with a serious look, "I don't know about the honorable part, but never the less, I am Willie Williams. I am so pleased to have the opportunity to meet you young people. I know that you probably see this as a boring evening, but it's an important evening. Not just because we are going to give you a job, and let you make a little money, but because you are going to learn how to make money in America, as a black man. I don't mean that stuff on TV with the singers, sports players, and dope boys. As Mr. Williams said dope boys the men instantly looked at each other smiling, as they shook their hand clapping.

Mr. Williams waited patiently for the men to stop clapping, as he looked seriously piercing down at each of us. I don't have all the answers, but what I know, I can share with you. You cannot go forward, if you do not give back. Be careful how you treat people on your way up, because you have to see the same people, on your way down. And at the end, may your works, speak for you. Every person born, whether old man or young man has a destiny, he was born to fulfill. Each person has a calling that was placed on his life by God, before he was conceived. To whom much is given, much is expected. Everything you have is a gift from God, a tool to be used to contribute to the body of Christ and do God's will. This means the gifts of knowledge, wealth, influence, or any other gift, are merely tools, to be used to ooze the character of heaven on to this world. Therefore, it is imperative, that people with gifts, give and teach the youth to have a spirit to receive. But not just receive these worldly gifts, but also understand the importance of giving.

I can remember when I was growing up, my father died when I was nine years old. I had older brothers who were off in the military, so as most boys did, I had to learn it, and how I live it. But, next door to me lived a man by the name of Mr. Jack Jones. Mr. Jones was what I call a real man. He didn't run over to the house when my father died trying to be my Daddy. He just watched me, and one day he saw me outside raking leaves. He walked over and asked me if I wanted a job. From that day on, I worked with Mr. Jones. From that old man, I learned everything about being a man. I learned about customer service, and how to deal with situations, like a gentlemen. I learned how to manage money. Mr. Jones would talk to me about inventory and sales, and how to ensure profits and how to redirect profits, for more profits. But most of all, I learned how a man of integrity, should be for the people. I watched as Mr. Jones gave his time to community outreach programs, and his money and resources to different organizations without hesitation. Mr. Jones continued to succeed as he taught me, and other young men, and gave to the community, and displayed to me, what a father should be.

I look back at this man, and I say what if he had not reached out to me. I tell you who would have, what's on my corner, the Bloods, they would have or the Four Corner Hustlers. So now, I stand before you with a debt that I owe, and I plan to pay. And that's all I got to say."

Chapter Twenty-Nine

BETTER DAYS

D addy came home from work happy nothing like he used to be. You can tell that Daddy feels like a man now. "I am tell you baby in three years we will have enough money to start up the business. All we have to do is keep saving. Mr. Lawson told me that's how he started out. He even said he would help me to start the business up. Daddy stated as he smiled from ear to ear. Momma just looked and smiled shaking her head as she prepared the chicken. Daddy then looked at me. "Lewis I am trying to get the business started so you and you can work for me and then go to college. I don't want you to end up like me hustling in the streets. If I had known how easy it was to start a business when I was your age it's no telling where I would be."

Daddy then pointed towards the cabinets he was building in the front room. Daddy is building custom cabinets in his spear time. "You see these cabinets son I am going to use the money I get from these to purchase lawn care equipment. When you make extra money you have to take it and invest it in things which make money. That's the only way to make money in America. Nobody is going t let you get rich working for them. If you want to get make money you have to have your own business."

Momma bought the chicken to the table as I instantly grabbed a piece. As I bit the greasy chicken my mouth began to blow attempting to adjust to the heat from the chicken. I could taste the mouth warming taste of ranch as I bit down on the chicken. Between bits I stated, "I know one thing one business that will work is opening up a restaurant for Momma, she must be the best cook in the world". The compliment put a smile on Mommas face that shined brighter than the moon on a dark night. Daddy then looked at the chicken and grabbed a piece himself as he stated, "That I must agree your chicken is finger licking good. We may need to find a spot and call it Momma's Fried Chicken." Alisha then jumped in Daddy's lap and then stated, "Daddy if we open a restaurant I want to take the orders." Daddy then pinched her nose and stated, "That sounds great I know you will write all the orders correct." My brother Brian then chimed in of course, "I want to work in the restaurant to Daddy can I be security." You sure can son Daddy stated as he winked at my brother." It was like my Daddy was a different person since he got this job the clouds of pain and suffering are gone from the family. They have been replaced with the sunshine of happiness and blessings. Daddy now smiles and dreams as all souls need to live. To Mr. Lawson he probably felt like he gave Daddy a job but he gave Daddy life.

As we ate the food I heard a knock at the door. I instantly jumped up Daddy looked at me and stated, "Lewis don't answer the door let your Momma answer." Momma then went to the door and gentlemen walked up with flowers and candy. He handed them to my mother as she looked them over in shock. Momma smiling with all of her teeth showing as she took the card looked over at my father and began to read the card.

Thank you for always being my sunshine during the storm. I love you very much.

Momma and all of us instantly walked outside with Momma and turned the corner outside of the apartment to find a shiny used SUV with Mommas name on the front plate. Momma was so happy as well as us. Momma grabbed Daddy and hugged him as Alisha and Brian began to climb in the backseat. Daddy then stated go ahead and get in the truck drive it to the park." We all then jumped in the car.

Chapter Thirty

WELCOME BACK JASON

Jason has finally come back to school from the alternative school. I feel kind of happy since I now have one of my boys back at the school. But I am also kind of scared, because I don't know what's going on with Jason these days. It's like he is not even the same person. He is doing drugs, boosting clothes, and skipping school. Even though I still consider him my friend, I don't really have any thing in common with him anymore. I know people pick on me. In fact, the only reason people in the neighborhood hang around me is, that Jason is my friend. But lately, it seems like every time I get around Jason, I end up getting in some type of trouble. But I don't feel right telling him no, since I feel like I owe him for taking up for me. But I also know, what Mr. Willis and the Black Men Conference has been teaching me about making good choices.

Jason is back and of course, the hall is stirred, thinking something is going to pop off. Everyone knows what happened at the skating ring, and they know that stuff like that is never over. It may die down for a little bit, but everybody wants to protect their swag. When you are a student at my school, your swag means everything. I just hope nothing pops off, because Marvin and I kind of swashed everything. Since we been in the program together, me and Marvin have actually been cool, but of course, we have to make it seem like we are in conflict in public, why I don't know.

So far during the day everything had been tense, but still no trouble. I tried to stay away from Jason and his groupies on the way from class. I could see Jason smiling as a few guys followed him each period to the restroom. I could see Marvin and his crew, mean mugging them every period, as Jason walked around with a smirk, as if to say, let's do it, we are ready when you are.

The bell rang for connections. As we started to walk down the hall, Jason stated to me, "Man, who do you have for connections?" I then stated, "I have P.E why do you ask?" Jason looked at me smiling, with his I am about to get in trouble smile. I have come to know now. "Man, we are about to duck off into the bathroom and skip class." Now in my head, I am thinking, why would someone want to skip class? What are you going to do, sit in a stinky bathroom and hide from security, what is the use? I then stated, "Man I don't think you should skip class, you just got back to school, and I got P.E so I know I am going to class." Jason then got excited, "All man you got P.E that's good, now you can sneak me in." I looked at him like he was crazy, "Man I can't do it, what if they catch me? I can't afford to get in any more trouble." Jason then started his same old tricks, trying to convince me to follow him. "Man come on, all you have to do is walk over when they throw the balls out, and push the door when I walk up."

I thought about it for a minute. Lately, every time I am around Jason it seems that I am getting in trouble and doing things I normally wouldn't do. I also thought about what Daddy and Mr. Willis said about making the right decisions. "No, man I can't do it." Jason then looked at me all crazy with a mean look, he stated, "Man, we supposed to be boys, every time you need me, I am there. When someone tries to jump you, who has your back and when you need clothes, who helps you? Man every since you started hanging with this teacher, you been acting real lame." I thought about it. Jason was right; he had my back since day one, so I have to have his back. With hesitation, I started shaking my head with an unsure look, "Ok man, I will open the door for you."

Once I made it to the gym, I sat in the bleachers directly next to the door. I waited until the students were all dressed out. The coaches were occupied giving the students their groups and balls. I then opened the door, letting Jason and two other knuckle heads, which are always in trouble, Leon and Robert in. They ran directly into the bathroom. The whole time I am thinking, why would you skip class to try to get into another class? But I didn't think anything of it since most of the time; people try to sneak into the gym to play basketball or hideout. It is hard to detect students in the gym since it is so many students. After about fifteen minutes, I noticed Jason and the other two boys had run out of the gym. After, about ten minutes I saw them run out of the restroom, and they exited the gym.

After about thirty minutes Coach Milton blew the whistle, "Alright everyone go dress in for today." We then ran into the locker room. The minute we make it to the restroom I heard someone yell out, "Man somebody stole my wallet and my phone." People that had forgotten to leave their stuff with Coach Milton instantly began searching. Sure enough, all their stuff had been stolen. Someone instantly ran out to get Coach Milton. Coach Milton came into the restroom looking upset. Coach Milton is a big man who is overweight, but a good football coach. Most of the time Coach is cool, but you know when he is mad because his eyebrows connect and his eyes get tight. Mr. Milton then states in his drill sergeant voice, "I am only going to say this one time, whoever has the items you can make it easy on yourself and give them up now. I am about to call Officer Wilkins and he will search everyone in this locker room. Also, we are going to roll back the cameras. So there is no way around it, you will be caught."

People then began to look around. One kid accused another kid then stated, "Man don't try me, I didn't steal anything I am not a junkie!" Another kid walked around with his fist balled yelling, "Somebody is going to give me back my stuff or it's going to be some problems." Mr. Milton then stated, "I need everyone to take a seat and remain quiet until Mr. Wilkins gets here. He is viewing the cameras."

The entire time I was thinking what am I going to do? Daddy just talked to me about Jason and making better decisions. Daddy is going to kill me. First I thought about snitching and telling the truth that I didn't know what was about to go down. Then I thought about what if they still take me down with them or worse if people find out I am a snitch. And lastly what would happen to Jason if I snitched. All of a sudden the intercom came on, "Coach Milton, you may let them go, we have the guys who did it here in the office." I instantly began smiling shaking my head. Man that was a close one. But this is it I am finished with Jason. Yes, Jason helped me out a couple of times, and we been friends a long time. But it's time to let this dude make it.

Chapter Thirty-One

THE SHOOT OUT

I hadn't seen Jason in about a week every since the incident in the gym. Jason and the other boys were suspended for ten days pending a hearing. With Jason's tract record this meant he was probably going to be placed back in alternative school. As I am on my way from school to work Jason and his crew came up out of no were riding in a Jaguar. Jason was riding in the back and hollered out, "What's up L, man are you going to ride with us, we about to go to the Westside?" Jason stated as he jumped out of the car with eyes blood shot red. Big O was driving while Jason sat in the front and his follower; Robert was in the back seat. I just looked at them and shook my head. I had given up on Jason changing. I was starting to see that Daddy was right. Some people just want do right. I then stated, "Man I have some work to do; I have to make this money." Jason then stated as he jumped around smiling, "Man why you cleaning up for these rich people, we getting ready to go get paid. I guess you and your Daddy can come and work for us." All of the other guys instantly started laughing. Jason could tell by the look on my face I was pissed off at him. I looked at him with disbelief. I couldn't believe he said that. I just looked at him and shook my head then stated, "Man Jason, man you are getting grimier every day. I don't care what you say about my Daddy, at least I got one." Next thing I knew I saw a look in Jason face I had never saw him direct at me, but I had witnessed this look when he dealt with other people, so I knew what time it was. Suddenly, Jason rushed towards me looking evil, like he was ready to kill me. Jason ran up to me and punched me in the face, before I knew it, I was on the ground. Jason then started kicking and stomping me, as he yells, "Man you not my boy, you know my Daddy dead." Next thing I knew everyone started pulling Jason off of me, "Come on man, leave that little faggot along, you know we are in a hot box, Robert stated." Jason jumped in the car, as I looked up blood was streaming from my eye I could hardly see Jason's face. I knew Jason was sorry for what he had done, but I knew, he was lost and confused.

A couple of men who were standing in front of the store walked over as they sped away. One of them an old man, who looked like either a junkie or an alcoholic stated, "You alright, young blood?" I stated, "Yes, I'm alright, I'll be alright sir." I then walked into the store to use the restroom. I could see that my face was still bleeding slightly and that my right eye was swollen. I rinsed out my lower eye until I could no longer see blood coming out and then started back towards work. I knew Daddy would be angry with me being late, but with a swollen eye I knew he would forget all about punctuality. Daddy had already explained to me, the penalty for being late. Each minute I am late, I knew would cost me fifty cents. This meant that by the time I made it to the house, I was looking at three dollars.

As I walked in the house, my father could hear me walking in and stated, "You are late, you know that it will be deducted from your pay. The minute my father walked in the room, he immediately noticed my eye, "What happened to your eye? Did you get into a fight or something?" I was so ashamed I didn't know what to say. I was actually kind of embarrassed; it is hard to tell your father, you lost a fight. I stated, "I got into a little fight on my way from school'" Daddy held my face, looking at my eye, "It looks like you got the bad side of this fight. What were you fighting about?" I didn't want to tell Daddy that I got into a fight with Jason. Since me and Jason were supposed to be friends, plus Daddy had already warned me to stop hanging around him. I didn't want Daddy to know the truth, so I lied. "I was at the basketball court, and I got in an argument with this kid from the south side, which was older." I tried not to look at Daddy as I talked, turning my head. I always feel uncomfortable lying to my parents. The crazy part about it, I always feel like they can look at me and tell when I am lying.

Daddy then stated, "I been talking with Mr. Lee Chi, and he told me I could sign you up for his karate classes. Do you think that's something you would be interested in?" I instantly began envisioning me, kicking people like they do in the karate movies. As I stated, "Yes, that's something I definitely would like to learn to do." "Well alright, I will check into it tomorrow, now let's get down to business," Daddy stated with a smile as he handed me the broom. I started sweeping the room while Daddy was in the other room treating the floors. Daddy always leaves the radio playing while we are working. It's always on 77.5, the station that plays the grown folks music, as Daddy calls it, or the old school, as I call it. As we worked all of a sudden, the even news spot came in.

"We come to give you up to date news of a robbery which occurred in Balk town. Four teenagers were involved in a robbery, which resulted in two of the teens being killed and two critically injured in a shoot out, in an attempted robbery at a downtown store. The police have not identified the boys who were reported, to be driving in a stolen Jaguar."

Instantly, my heart dropped, I couldn't believe it. Could it be Jason and the other boys had been killed? Before I knew it, I blurted out, "Ah man, Ah man," as I ran into the room were Daddy was working with my eyes bucked in disbelief. "Daddy, Daddy did you hear what they said on the radio? I think that might be Jason, Daddy I have to go!" I stated as Daddy looked at me confused, wondering what I was talking about.

Daddy stated, "How do you know that it was Jason?" I stated, "I saw Jason earlier, riding earlier with some other dudes in a Jaguar." Daddy then looked at me and shook his head. "Ok, let's ride over to the complex and check with Jason's Mom." As we rode, it seemed like a small four block drive, took forever.

When we pulled up to the apartment, I looked over at Jason's door and I didn't see anyone. I saw Jason's next door neighbor, Rodney. Rodney was standing outside working on his bike. Rodney is known around the neighborhood for working on bicycles, but most of all, for doing tricks on bicycles. The minute I walked up Rodney stated, "Man, he is not here, the police called. Jason got shot, and his whole family is up at the hospital." I ran back down stairs where

Daddy was waiting. "Come on, let's ride up to the National Hospital and check on him."

When we made it to the hospital, police were standing in front of the room Jason was in. His mom and brothers were standing out in the front. I could tell that Miss. Williams had been crying and her eyes were red and puffy. Jason's mom and her boyfriend sat next to her trying to comfort her. "Hello Mrs. Williams, I was just coming by to check on Jason." Mrs. Williams then stated, "He is still in the operating room." I looked at Daddy and he just took a seat. This let me know, that we could wait for them to finish the operation. We waited. I listened to his brothers discussing what happened. After Jason and the boys drove away they decided to go jacking. One of the boys Donald, better known as Big O, had a gun. Donald was about seventeen but loved to hang around younger boys that he knew would look up to him. Donald, Jason, and the other, Robert, went into the jewelry store down town and attempted to rob the store. They had planned to take the money and the jewelry. The problem was when they went in, they didn't know that the owner was in the back and heard the whole thing. The owner called the police and then grabbed his gun. This was not an ordinary gun but an assault rifle. The man came out with rifles and start firing. Robert got killed and Big O, and Jason are in critical condition.

After about four hours the doctor came out. He said that Jason had been shot in the back and that he would be paralyzed. The doctors said they are still not certain if Jason would be able to walk again.

Chapter Thirty-Two

THE CONTEST

Treion, Marvin and I decided to join the school drama club. Of course, it was after much persuasion by Mr. Willis and B-Lo. Also, when Mr. Vinson came to speak, that really motivated us. Mr. Vinson came to speak to us when we went to the student African American leadership conference. Mr. Vinson told us how, even when he was a young boy, he also wanted to be an actor and writer. He told us about how he got his start acting in the church plays. Mr. Vinson said that by the time he was twelve, he was asked to help write the Easter service that year. Mr. Vinson stated, "Out of all the applauses I have ever received, all across the world, no applause made me happier than that standing ovation I got, after writing that little church play. From that moment on, Mr. Vinson said he knew what he wanted to do. And just look at him now, he has more money than anyone in entertainment. I mean he has the chance to get money like Oprah.

Marvin and Treion were excited about acting, but I knew that wouldn't fit my personality. I can't act, because I get nervous when I speak in class doing presentations. But, I can write. I talked to Mr. Kilkenny or Mr. K as everyone calls him, about writing a strip for the play. Mr. K informed me that the script was going to be chosen by the entire club, but that anyone could write a script in relations to Civil Rights. Whoever had the best script would be chosen for the up incoming school play for Black History Month. The first thing everyone thinks about when they think about Civil Rights is how people treated African-Americans in the past, and how they fought for Civil Rights. But when I went to the library I found out that Civil Rights are just rights given to every person as a human, freedom from discrimination, prejudice and inequality. Still I couldn't think what to write about.

I thought about it for a couple of days, and then I was in the lunchroom sitting, thinking. Man it's only three days left before the scripts are due for submission, and I don't have anything. Then I looked around the cafeteria, and it came to me. Over here, you have the popular kids or kids with swag sitting. They all have on name brand clothes and look good. They seem happy and think, they think that they are all that. They all sit at the end of the tables smiling and laughing. These are the kids that always joke other kids that don't dress like them, or don't have the looks, that they were blessed with. A few of them are cool, seem to be cool but they still laugh at jokes people make against other people.

On the other side sitting off to in the corner rows alone, you have the gay boys and girls who kind of sit off by themselves. For some reason, the girls don't get picked on as much as the boys. The boys are the guys that people really joke, since they don't act like other boys, they are automatically outcast. People joke them about being gay, fagots, and sweet. Some might be gay and some might be soft spoken either way, they are all still lumped the same way. Just because they may not like sports or talk like other boys, they really get picked on. These guys are normal topics for jokes, even by the lowest of the school circle. People don't want to be seen with them, out of fear of being joked or guilty by association.

Then you got my group, the dirty boys. We don't have the clothes or the looks, so we kind of get viewed as lame. Most of us just hang out, and talk and joke with each other during lunch. We don't have the money for expensive clothes. Most of us are in little clicks, and we look out for each other. People might joke us, but they know that if they take go too far, we will fight. We are just below the groupies, so we are the lames as they call it.

The majority of the people are the groupies. They are not considered popular, but they are not considered lame either. They keep the popular people popular by laughing when they pick on other kids. They are always trying to figure out how they can move up the popularity chart. They get picked on sometimes, but only, by the popular kids. But they get to take out their pain on the kids considered lame.

But as I looked at all these groups, I saw the last group, the ungrouped. These are the special education students. These kids don't get picked on in their faces, but they get picked on every day in another way. Every time someone calls another person retarded, that is rude towards the disabled students. Every time a person laughs at someone, or makes a joke about a situation, that disabled kids can't control. They make horrible jokes, like mental or physical disability cracks that is wrong too. I often wondered how a person could look at a handicapped person and laugh, I always felt sad for them.

After looking at all of the injustice at Marcus Garvey Middle School, I realized that I didn't need to try to focus on Civil Rights from the text book or history. We have discrimination going on at my school against people based on their looks, sexual orientation, income and even disabilities. I realized that the students of today make the citizens of tomorrow. I started thinking, if we want the world to be different in the future, then we have to start changing how we treat each other, because we are the future.

Then I came up with an idea but I didn't know what Mr. Vinson would say. I just wanted to do something different, that related to civil rights, according to what kids deal with. Also, I didn't know how people would view the play. I was thinking more than likely, this will just make people joke about me even more.

When I presented the play, everyone in the class including Mr. Vinson was speechless. The first thing I am thinking is, old boy, here we go. But Mr. Vinson instead stated, "Looks like the competition is over. We pretty much know who the winner of the contest is, for this school. Good job Lewis, I think you have a chance to win the entire contest, are there any objections?" Everyone smiled and began congratulating me. Even Marvin was like, "Man, you might end up the next Tyler Perry, for real".

Chapter Thirty-Three

THE PLAY

I could not believe everyone is making such a big deal about this play. I was so nervous; all my life I have never won any award. And now I am receiving a scholarship, my name is going in the paper over a school play. Daddy and Momma were so excited that they let Alisha and Brian miss school to see the play. A lot of the men from the program are coming as well. I was asked to do the narrator's part and Marvin is playing the main character. I am nervous I don't know why, but I begin the play anyway.

Scene I Nightmare at Garvey

Narrator: As James walked into the school he walked up to his crew as normal. James is one of the so called in crowd. This consists of James and his crew, who is all well liked by the girls at the school and play sports. They enjoy their early morning routine of sitting in the restroom, making jokes about other boys, and bullying them. Today something is different. When James walks in the restroom to see his crew as they are busy making jokes about two other boys in the hallway while other people are around laughing, James walks up to join in on the joking session of Carlos. He instantly begins laughing, thinking of how he can join in on joking Carlos, about the pink pants he has on and for being gay. James walks up laughing, ready to join in talks, but he does not know that he is no longer in the in-crowd. He does not have the good looks, he once had or the nice clothes. He is now just like one of the kids, he likes to pick on. This is his worst nightmare.

James: Look at that little girl with those pink pants.

Narrator: James friend looks at James like, who is this guy?

Jame's Friend one—Look at his clown. He is trying to joke with all of those bumps on his face.

Narrator: James looks around confused, wondering who is this his friend is talking about?

In crowd boy two—He wants to laugh at sweet pea but look at him. At least sweet pea has some shoes. Look at his shoes he is so lame!!

Narrator: The crowd instantly began to laugh as the boys and girls laugh and point at his shoes.

James bucks his eyes in disbelief.

In-Crowd II Boy Two—I can't believe this clown came to school with those clothes on and then he has the nerve to try to joke someone.

James—Mark what' up, man?

Mark—What's up is your flooding pants lame?

Narrator: James looks around confused as everyone laughs at him. James can't take the embarrassment so he quickly runs to the restroom as the crowd continues to joke him and point at him. James can't believe it when he looks in the mirror to find that he is dressed in a very uncool shirt and that his face has bumps and his hair cut looks crazy. James runs out of the restroom screaming and runs to the custodian's room to hide. James bumps into a wall and falls asleep.

As James sleeps he has a dream. A ghost appears from nowhere in his dreams while he is in the closet.
James: Who are you? What do you want?
Ghost: I am the Ghost of Civil Rights. I came to show you that everyone should have rights so follow me.

Scene II The Future

Narrator: The ghost leads James to the front of a school. The Ghost leads James to the gym were a memorial is being held.
James: Man, that is my school. Why are we here?
Ghost: Don't ask questions. Just go in the school.

Students, we are at Marcus Garvey Middle School for a memorial to honor a student who committed suicide. He was a wonderful child, born with a passion for people. All Carlos wanted to do was make people around him happy. Carlos loved band, making people laugh, math and his fellow students. You could often see Carlos before class helping students to complete homework assignments and make-up. Carlos would even help students that he knew made jokes about him on a daily basis because he was different. Who can forget Carlos with his saxophone playing at all of the assemblies? Carlos always had a smile on his faith and would always make everyone feel good when around him.

Carlos was a straight A student who dreamed of completing a degree at Morehouse College in engineering. Carolos would often tell his mother, "Momma, one day I am going to be an engineer and inventor and buy you a big house." See Carlos's life revolved around helping other people. But enough about my thoughts about Carlos because I think we all know who he was. I came here today to honor his last request. Carlos requested that we read this letter to the whole school and that's what we are here for.

Carlos to the World: *As I write my last letter I would like to say to my friends and families don't cry for me. I am going to a better place. I had to leave this world so that I could be free. Free to be me and accepted to go somewhere beautiful where being me is not hated. I am going somewhere where people don't pick on you and call you names just because you are different. I am going somewhere that Martin Luther King talked about in his," I Have a Dream speech. Where people are not judged by their sexuality, looks, or clothes, but by their character, that is where I am going.*

Many days I would smile as people would say stuff about me, but I was really dying on the inside. Plenty of days I would sit up at night praying to God that people would accept me for me and stop picking on me. After a while I got tired of the hell of this world and I had to plan to leave this world. I am ready to go to a world I visited every night in my dreams. I am going to a world where people who are different are not treated badly for being different, and I will be so happy. So don't cry for me because I am going somewhere happier, and I don't have to be stressed out. But, please remember this world does not have to be hell for anyone. If people could start to put themselves in the shoes of another person, and accept people who are different, then finally this world can become a better place. So like Dr. King, I may not get there with you, but I know that one day we will overcome and every person: gay, straight, ugly, pretty, rich, poor, cool or lame will be able to be treated fair and have happiness.

Principal: Now that you have heard Carlos's letter, we will now play a song.

Narrator: The crowd begins to play "We Shall Over Come"

As James saw the funeral he instantly looks over at the ghost with tears in his eyes.

James: I am so sorry. I was just joking with Carlos, but I didn't mean any harm.

Ghost of Civil Rights: You didn't mean to hurt, but you still did.

James: What can I do to make it right?

Ghost of Civil Rights: You can not control the past, but you can change the future.

James-What does that mean?

Scene III Back to the Present

Narrator: The ghost then begins to vanish. James then began to scream, as he awakes from his dream and runs to the restroom.

James looks in the mirror, and he is backed to looking handsome.

The bell then begins to ring, and people start to come into the restroom.

Friend—What's up man, guess who just came in the restroom? Its old sweet pants.

The other friends began to crowd around the boy laughing ready to start joking him.

Friend II—Now sweet pants, you know you are in the wrong restroom.

Friend Three—I guess I am going to have to slap some sense into this faggot.

Other boys begin to crowd around laughing and pointing as Carlos looks sad.

James immediately jumps between the boys.

James—Leave this dude along.

Friend II—Man James, what's up man, you are tripping?

James—No, man, you are tripping. Treat people like you want to be treated. Regardless of someone's sexual preference, they are still human, so you don't have the right to make them feel bad

Narrator—Now that you have heard the conclusion of this play, let the lesson learned by James be a lesson learned by you. Bullying is not cool. When you laugh or stand around while another person is being bullied, it's still wrong. Treat people like you want to be treated and we can all share in the dream Dr. King envisioned of a world where everyone is treated equally. During that time, they fought for equality: regardless of race, religion, creed or color. Today we must fight for equality, regardless of sexual orientation, physical appearance or social economic background. Every day we can keep the dream alive by fighting the good fight against bullies and people who treat people unfair. Whether fat, skinny, pretty, ugly, gay or straight please let's stop the hate.

When the narrator finished, the crowd instantly jumped up clapping. Everyone in the gym was standing.

Mr. Vinsion finally came up as the cast continued to smile and take their applause. Mr. Vinison began on the microphone, "If I could get everyone's attention please, please. I would like to just highlight the author of this play and the recipient of the American Cola Scholarship, Mr. Lewis Williams.

The crowd began to cheer louder as I stepped to the podium, embarrassed by all of the attention. As I looked in the crowd, I could see Tiffany clapping as she looked directly my way. For a moment, I imagined it was just me and Tiffany in the room, and she was just smiling at me.

After the ovation, people could not wait to flood towards me with compliments and congratulations. I stood around embarrassed as I received compliment from students that normally only insult me, as several men from the program continued to compliment, as Momma and Daddy just stood there smiling. But I couldn't believe it, when standing in a cluster directly in front of me, I saw Tiffany eyeing me down smiling as she giggled with her friends.

I couldn't believe it, but after a moment it looked like she was walking my way. I kept telling myself she is not coming over here, she is just passing by. All of a sudden Tiffany is standing directly in front of me smiling. My heart is beating, and I am wondering what in the world am I going to say or for that matter, what she is going to say. Tiffany then stated,

"I enjoyed your play. I wanted to talk to you about the letter you wrote. I really liked the letter I was just waiting for you to approach me. I would not mind going out with you." I didn't know what to say. Tiffany must have known, she just looked at me and smiled and stated, here is my number, call me later."

Daddy then walked up and stated, "So is this the young lady you have been talking about." I wanted to sink into the ground I was so embarrassed but Tiffany just smiled and stated, "My name is Tiffany please to me you sir. Well I see you later Lewis," Tiffany stated as she walked back to her friends. I could not believe how my life has changed in the last six months. For the first time in my life it seems like the storm is over and the sunshine has come out.

About the Author

Jimmie R. McKnight, PhD (ABD) is a native of Mound Bayou, Mississippi. He is a motivational speaker and a consultant. He is also an educator on both the collegiate and secondary level. He attended Delta State University where he earned a B.S in Social Science. He also earned a Masters of Art in Political Science from Mississippi State University. He is currently in the completion stages of his dissertation to earn a Doctoral of Philosophy in Political Science from Clark Atlanta University. He is a member of Alpha Phi Alpha Fraternity, Inc. His goal is to see the Empowerment Program empower at-risk youth all over America.